"Worth the trip?" Tom asked, putting his arm around me.

"It's beautiful," I whispered, taking in the view of the village and the surrounding countryside.

"And I think you're beautiful," Tom murmured as he turned to face me. He put his other arm around my waist and pressed me to him before he covered my mouth with his lips.

I wanted that kiss to go on forever, but I knew I should break away. "We'd better go in," I said breathlessly.

Dear Readers,

We at Silhouette would like to thank all our readers for your many enthusiastic letters. In direct response to your encouragement, we are now publishing *three* FIRST LOVEs every month.

As always FIRST LOVEs are written especially for and about you—your hopes, your dreams, your ambitions.

Please continue to share your suggestions and comments with us; they play an important part in our pleasing you.

I invite you to write to us at the address below:

Nancy Jackson
Senior Editor
Silhouette Books
P.O. Box 769
New York, N.Y. 10019

THREE WEEKS OF LOVE
Patricia Aks

First Love from Silhouette

Published by Silhouette Books New York

America's Publisher of Contemporary Romance

SILHOUETTE BOOKS, a Simon & Schuster Division of
GULF & WESTERN CORPORATION
1230 Avenue of the Americas, New York, N.Y. 10020

Copyright © 1983 by Patricia Aks

Distributed by Pocket Books

ISBN: 0-671-53347-9

First Silhouette Books printing May, 1983

10 9 8 7 6 5 4 3 2 1

America's Publisher of Contemporary Romance

Printed in the U.S.A.

For Tom and his parents, Carol and Richard
For my English friends, Micha, Gilda and Michael, whose hospitality knows no bounds
For David, with thanks for providing so many details
And for Harold, without whom none of this would have been possible, my love and gratitude

THREE
WEEKS OF
LOVE

1

Don't you think Saxe is overdoing it?" Daisy asked as we trudged down the stairs of our school after a full day of rehearsal.

"Has to," I defended. "He warned us in the fall that if the madrigal group was serious about going to England this summer, we had to work like crazy."

"True, but I guess I blocked out the fact that we'd be doing nothing this last week but rehearse. School's out, but I'm busier than ever. This routine is interfering with my love life."

"What do you mean?"

"Last night I had a date with Greg, but I was so exhausted I conked out at ten o'clock."

"I hope you fell asleep in his arms, at least."

We had arrived at the exit and Daisy, who was about to push open the front door, stopped cold in her tracks and stared at me. "You really are a mind reader, Beth. I couldn't keep a secret from you even if I wanted to."

"Then you did fall asleep in his arms."

"Of course," she said, and we both giggled.

Even though we're sixteen, hardly infants, we have a very low threshold when it comes to giggling, especially when we talk about boys. Daisy, however, has more to offer in this department than I do because she's always in love. Usually her romances are short-lived—lasting longer than chicken pox, but shorter than mononucleosis—which is the way she describes them. But her recent involvement with Greg, a junior who's a photography freak and can cream Daisy at tennis, one of her requirements for falling in love had lasted four weeks and was still going strong. Daisy admitted there was an intensity to their relationship because they would be separated all summer. Greg was going to be a counselor in Maine and would leave before we returned from England.

"There we were, sitting in his rec room, listening to a new Olivia Newton-John record album, and zap, I was out like a light," Daisy continued. "I was so embarrassed."

"Nothing to be embarrassed about if you didn't snore," I said.

"I never thought of that!" she exclaimed, and then we both cracked up again.

Daisy and I have been friends since seventh grade, and I suppose one of the reasons we get along so well is because we're not really competitive. She's number three on the tennis team, and will probably be the best in the school by the time she's a senior. I, on the other hand, am a real spaz when it comes to sports. Daisy couldn't understand why I had such difficulty on the tennis court, and she even tried hitting some balls to me early one morning last summer on the public courts when nobody was around. After a half hour of me slapping the ball into the net, or out of the court completely, she finally conceded that I was hopeless.

"Stick to singing," she advised. "You can't be a virtuosa at everything."

That was typical of Daisy—making me feel better by mentioning my one real passion in life—music, and singing, especially. Daisy knows that, and always tells me how lucky I am that I have a built-in talent.

"But you do, too," I insist whenever we get into one of our 'what will we do in life?' discussions. "You're a terrific tennis player."

"So when it comes to careers, you'll be a diva at the Met, and I'll be a tennis pro." After discussing the pros and cons of such possibilities, we always end up laughing, which is one of the reasons our friendship has survived four stormy years. I mean there's nothing like having a sense of humor when all else fails, and Daisy and I invariably see the funny side of life.

I've told Daisy she has the most appropriate name in the world because she's cute, and fresh, and wears well. She claims she hated it as a little kid because she didn't like being named after a flower. But her mother, who is a bit ditsy, explained that flowers ran in the family—her name is Rose—and with a last name like Smith, something memorable was in order. Now Daisy agrees, which she says is a sign of her maturity. Also, she looks like a daisy: pert, blond, and smiley. We are exactly the same height, five-four, but there the resemblance ends. Unlike Daisy, I'm built like an ironing board. My hair is on the long side, and dark, and I have gray eyes. Daisy tends to be round, her hair is short and wavy, and she has brown eyes.

We actually discovered each other in seventh grade as a result of an assignment in our communications class. Communications was an experimental course that included a smattering of psychology, among other things. Our teacher, Ms. Bevin, was fresh out of some school of education in the east. She wore horn-rimmed glasses, her hair was as frazzled as her manner, and she had a frantic air about her, but her class was never dull. She was always coming up with wild ideas and this time she was conducting an experiment to prove that personality traits can be determined by order of birth, that is, whether one is an older, middle, or younger child. We were asked to write our distinguishing characteristics and then compare our profiles with those similarly ranked.

It was an assignment everyone got into because, who doesn't like writing about themselves? But the best thing about it was that Daisy and I found out we were the only "onlys" in the class, used identical adjectives in describing ourselves—independent, sociable, lonely at times, pressured by parents—and at the end of our list, we both disclaimed being spoiled. Ms. Bevin said she couldn't draw any world-shaking conclusions from such a limited sample, but she showed us that there were definite characteristics shared depending where we were at in the family, and the most astounding similarity was between the two "only" children in the class. Since Daisy had just entered school in the seventh grade, having moved from Chicago, I had never gotten to know her. But after we discovered all the things we had in common, our friendship developed and we've been tight ever since.

We're very supportive of each other. She says she'll always be grateful to me for getting her interested in chorus, and sheepishly admits that it never occurred to her that she could sing.

"You don't have to be great, just good," I encouraged her. "And there's nothing like it."

It turned out she was better than good and even qualified for a place in the madrigal group, a small chorus of twenty-four, that boasts the best voices in the school. Daisy is an alto, which is fortunate for both of us, because we're not next to each other when we sing. Mr. Saxe—we wouldn't dare call him by his first name, Harry—is a perfectionist when it comes to music, but he keeps us off-balance with his outrageous antics during rehearsals. He looks a little like Walter Matthau, a younger version, but he's at least forty, and it's amazing that someone so shaggy looking can be so insistent on precision. By the time a rehearsal is over, his hair has flopped over his forehead, the shoelaces on his hush puppies are invariably untied, and his shirt is no longer tucked in. Yet, if our "attacks" and "cut-offs" aren't perfect, he shakes his head with despair and asks us if we're majoring in idiocy. On the other hand, if we do something that pleases him, he gets this beatific smile on his face that makes the verbal abuse we've endured worthwhile.

Sometimes he has us laughing so hard that if I were next to Daisy we'd both have to be carried out on a stretcher. One of our pieces is "The Lobster Quadrille" from *The Alice in Wonderland Suite* and Saxe's way of getting us into a crustacean mood is to waggle his fingers in the air and make lobster faces. Fortunately, he confines this kind of warm-up to rehearsals or we'd never get through the concert.

Singing with Saxe is super—just ask any member of the chorus—so you can imagine how ecstatic we were when we learned that the madrigal group might be going to England. Our school, Bryant High, in a suburb of Cleveland, is known for its trendy programs, even though it's a public school and is at least 100 years old. This would be the first time a trip across the ocean had been planned.

It all started because of Jeremy Rivers, an Englishman whose father had lost his life as a pilot with the RAF during World War II. Jeremy, as a small boy, had been evacuated to the United States with his mother, and they'd settled in Cleveland where they had a distant cousin. Jeremy eventually attended Bryant High School. He graduated from medical school, acquired dual citizenship, became a successful doctor and an active member in community projects. He never forgot his English roots, but he was unendingly grateful for the opportunities offered to him in America, especially Bryant High. He was asked to speak at Commencement a year ago. After hearing the madrigal chorus, which was part of the graduation program, he was inspired to sponsor a Hands Across the Sea program. Since Dr. Rivers was a descendant of Lord Jeremy Rivers, the founder of the Rivers Parish Church in England, what would be more fitting than to have the Bryant High School madrigal chorus sing there?

Actually, the madrigal chorus had been rehearsing once a week, in addition to our regular chorus rehearsals, in preparation for our English tour ever since September when it seemed possible that our dreams would become reality. But it wasn't until school was out, at the end of June, that we worked with such intensity. Daisy's not the only one who complained about Saxe's seven-seven discipline—seven hours of rehearsal, seven days a week.

"Don't worry, guys, I'm giving you ten-minute breaks every 100 minutes, in addition to a thirty-

minute lunch break," he announced at the beginning of
our first full day.

"Oh, Mr. Saxe," Sabrina whined. "That's not nearly
enough."

"You mean I'm being too easy. Maybe I should cut
down the lunch break?" he suggested, purposely misin-
terpreting her objection. Mr. Saxe is the only person I
know who is not buffaloed by Sabrina, who is a
perpetual complainer.

It's hard to understand why, because she is a tall,
blue-eyed blonde with a seductive manner who usually
gets her own way. At one point, I think every boy in the
class has had a crush on her. Daisy says Sabrina is a
phase every teenage boy must go through, like adoles-
cent skin. Now, fortunately, she's only interested in
college men, which leaves the field open to us lesser
mortals. Not that we haven't had our share of admirers,
but no girl in our class has left such a long trail of
broken hearts. No wonder she's snobby!

I soon discovered that practically everyone was
groaning about our schedule. I knew it was a case of
mob psychology, and underneath the surface of complaints each one of us knew the value of extending
ourselves. After all, we'd knocked ourselves out to
make the tour possible—raffles, concerts, cookie and
cake sales. We'd finally raised enough money and
nobody wanted to blow it at this late date. However, on
our lunch break during the fourth day of rehearsal, we
were all feeling the strain. A group of us clustered on
the benches surrounding the playground, and were
munching on bag lunches we'd brought from home.
The complaints reached a fever pitch.

"There'll be nothing left of my voice," Mike
groaned. Mike, a husky jock, looks more like a fullback

than a singer, and it came as a surprise that he had such a beautiful bass voice.

"You're not kidding," Patsy chimed in. Patsy, a member of the alto section, is funny, on the fat side, and has a cherubic face. "We'll be the most perfectly trained American high school chorus to ever grace foreign shores, and we won't be able to sing a note."

Then everyone, including Daisy, tried to outdo each other with clever remarks about the sacrifices we were making for art. I knew they were half-kidding, but I couldn't get into the spirit. I don't like feeling like an outsider, but there was no way I could fake the fact that I didn't believe wholeheartedly in what Mr. Saxe was trying to accomplish. I couldn't put it down, even jokingly.

I was relieved when the verbal jousts ended and it was time to get back to rehearsal. I didn't think anyone particularly noticed how quiet I'd been, but as we made our way back to the rehearsal room, Sabrina, who was several steps ahead of me, suddenly glanced back and said, "I suppose you don't agree, Beth? Nothing's too much for you."

I could feel myself bristle, but before I could answer, she had turned away and began talking to Andy, an undersized wimp who hung on to every word Sabrina uttered. I had hoped no one heard her because everyone would be on her side. Therefore, I was surprised when Peter, the accompanist for the chorus and an accomplished pianist, appeared at my side and muttered under his breath, "Don't let her bug you."

Peter and I rarely exchanged two words unless it had something to do with music. I could never decide whether he was shy, aloof, or indifferent. The only thing I knew about him for sure was that he was a serious musician who was going to Oberlin next year.

Peter was a nice guy, but I never thought about him especially. He was medium everything: medium-colored brown hair, medium tall, and medium good-looking. But his dark brown eyes, which I noticed for the first time, were amazingly warm and expressive, and his hands, with long, tapered fingers, were beautiful.

"I'll try not to," I said, as he smiled briefly and rushed past me. Shy, aloof, indifferent? I couldn't tell. All I knew for sure was that I could have hugged him for his support, Sabrina's remark had already faded into insignificance, and I could count on Peter to be on my side.

One of my biggest problems is that I always overreact to people and their opinions, good and bad. My father, Lewis, who's a trial lawyer, says I've got to toughen up or I'll never survive what life has to offer. He's very soft-spoken and gentle at home, and I was astounded when I first sat in on one of his court cases and how, in his quiet way, he demolished the prosecuting attorney.

My mother, Mary Beth, known as MB, is just the opposite. She covers her feelings with a layer of brisk-ness that's wafer thin. But I've been able to see through her ever since second grade. That was the time she found this abandoned kitten meowing in the backyard one morning before we'd even had breakfast. My father offered to take it to the pound, but my mother insisted it was "heaven-sent, we need a pet, and you know what will happen if it's not adopted in three days." Just saying those words brought tears to her eyes. It was the first time I ever saw my mother come close to crying, but I never forgot it.

Naturally, I was just as anxious as she was that we keep it and my father acquiesced. That's how Teeny, which is what we named her because she was so tiny and pitiful, came to be a member of our family. She turned into a scrumptious fat black cat, and my father suggested he legally change her name to Fatso. But MB, only half-kidding, said that might give her an identity crisis!

I look more like my father, except he's at least six feet tall, and wears wire-framed glasses. My mother is petite and very pretty. Her hair is pepper and salt, and she wears it short because, as she says, "I can't be bothered." Actually, she spends less time on her appearance than anyone I know, wears practically no makeup, but always looks great.

She and an old college friend, Erica, opened a needlepoint shop in our shopping mall three years ago, and my father says if it becomes any more successful he'll go into early retirement. The shop is called High Point, and Erica, who has twin boys in the sixth grade, claims it has saved her from lunacy. Erica is tall, gangly, disorganized, and looks as though she couldn't thread a needle, but her work is exquisite.

The idea for High Point started one day when Erica unexpectedly dropped in on my mother, who happened to be cleaning closets at the time. She noticed several needlepoint pillows, all various depictions of Teeny, that MB was stashing away. They discovered that they were both into needlepoint but there was never enough time to pursue their interest at home. "Why not set up shop?" Erica burst out, and my mother obviously thought it was a terrific idea because three months later they had leased a tiny store, lined the walls with bins that displayed a zillion different-colored skeins of wool, and they were in business. My father made all the legal arrangements, and Erica's husband, Jerry, a plump, good-natured, dynamite stockbroker, raised most of the money. He said it was just another risk, well worth taking, if it preserved Erica's sanity.

What I love about Erica is that she always treats me as an equal. Whenever I go to High Point, she can't wait to show me her latest original designs and describe the most recent escapades of the twins. She also shows a genuine interest in me, and when she learned from MB that the madrigal group was trying to raise money for the tour, she promptly offered some needlepoint patterns that could be sold, with the profits going to the cause. She designed a multi-colored clef sign that literally sold like hotcakes.

My mother also has magical fingers, which I did not inherit. That was proven shortly after High Point opened. I was thirteen years old then, and absolutely at my most sensitive. I had dropped over after school just when MB and Erica were closing up shop for the day. Their enthusiasm had rubbed off on me and I begged my mother to show me how it was done. MB tried to teach me the continental stitch, which is one of the easiest, but I kept making mistakes. She decided that we were proving the theory that mothers can't teach daughters anything, and turned me over to Erica. After watching my feeble attempts to follow her instructions and getting everything wrong, even Erica gave up on me. I couldn't seem to stay within the lines, my stitches were uneven, and I either pulled the thread too tight or too loose. My mother was straightening things, and purposely avoided interfering with my lesson, but finally Erica sighed, "You're right, MB, she's all thumbs."

My reaction was so bizarre, that an outsider observing the scene would have thought I'd been struck. Not only did I burst into tears, but I bolted out of the store and started running all the way home.

Erica was so upset that she raced after me, and when I stopped at a red light, she caught up with me.

"Honey, I'm sorry," she apologized breathlessly. "I didn't mean to hurt your feelings. I guess I'm too used to my kids. You'd have to run them over with a bulldozer in order for them to shed a tear!"

Erica was deadly serious, but I couldn't help smiling, and by the time she walked me back to the shop where my mother was still cleaning up, I had completely recovered. MB, who was accustomed to my unreasonable explosions, tactfully didn't say anything about the "incident," and went on about how they needed to order more shades of blue wool, because every woman who came in that day wanted something in the turquoise family. Neither Erica or my mother ever mentioned my futile attempt to learn needlepoint and I didn't pick up a needle, except to sew on buttons, for two years. Now I can laugh at myself for how I behaved that day, and I've learned to keep my tears under control, but I can't say that I still don't get hurt easily.

I also have to curb my excitement when someone compliments me. The first time I tried out for chorus in ninth grade, Mr. Saxe told me I was one of the best voices that had auditioned for him in three days. Since Saxe has a reputation for being hard to please, you would have thought I'd won a starring role in the Vienna Opera Company. When I came home that day and told my mother, she remarked, "That's nice, dear." I couldn't believe how tepid she was, and when I later informed my father, and all he said was, "Good for you," I was ready to leave home.

In retrospect, I realize that they were trying to protect me. I mean it's so easy to be disappointed, and that's not so apt to happen if you don't expect too much. It was just three measures of a German carol, but for me it took on all the aspects of an international debut. Even so, I was reluctant to try out for the soprano solo in the madrigal group. In the first place, the solos are almost always assigned to seniors or juniors, and in the second place, I wasn't ready to face rejection. But I was encouraged from all sides.

"You've got nothing to lose," Daisy pointed out. "You've got to take risks," my parents advised. But the final push came from Mr. Saxe, who announced when he would be having tryouts, and then added, "Don't be afraid of failure. If any of you are interested in a serious singing career, grab every possible opportunity to audition."

I knew he was talking to everyone in the chorus, but I couldn't help but think that his words were meant especially for me. Then he told us tryouts were scheduled for the following week. "Long enough to get your act together," he quipped. He was right about that, but he should have added that it was too long a time for us not to have a nervous breakdown, if that means not being able to think about anything else. If "cold feet" is an apt description of someone who's afraid, mine could have qualified as frigid. But I resisted backing down, if for no other reason than that I'd be called chicken.

I did psyche myself up, worked hard every day on mastering the Bach cantata, which was our tryout piece, and practiced what Saxe described as "a song of your own." I chose "I'll Never Walk Alone," which I hoped would show off my voice to its best advantage. By the time audition day arrived, I was prepared.

There were four of us trying out for the soprano solo, and as I anticipated, I was the only tenth-grader. I didn't know any of the other girls except through the chorus, because we didn't have any classes together, but I knew the competition was stiff. Priscilla had the lead role in *Guys and Dolls* the previous year, and had all the confidence of a pro. She was going to Bennington in the fall, and probably majoring in theater and voice. She swished around in full skirts and black turtlenecks and wore her long black hair in a single braid. Priscilla seemed totally unconcerned with other people's opinions and although I admired her, she scared me a little.

Helene, a junior, is small, dark, vivacious, and a non-stop talker. She stood next to me in chorus, and I was amazed that her voice was so big. As we waited outside the rehearsal room, Helene rattled on about being prepared for an execution, how glad she'd be when the ordeal was over, and wasn't there some less barbaric way of selecting a soloist. I was happy there was someone who felt the way I did, but I was too tense to kid around.

Greta, the fourth candidate, looks like a startled doe all the time, so it was hard to tell if she was frightened or not. She has large, innocent dark eyes, pale skin, sand-colored hair and a slender build that makes her appear deceptively fragile.

Greta was the first one summoned by Mr. Saxe. He stuck his head out the door and pointed at her. She bounced up and darted into the room while he held the door. Then he said, "You'll be next, Pris, then Beth, and then Helene."

He closed the door before he could hear Helene groan, "Just my luck to be last."

"It's not the end of the world," Priscilla remarked.

"I know it's not," Helene snapped. "I personally can't figure out why you two are so cool."

"Strictly a front," I admitted.

"Well, you're a very good actor. I wish I could pretend not to care."

"We can't all be chosen, so why don't you just relax," Priscilla advised.

"I wish I could!" Helene was getting more and more shrill.

"Why don't we talk about something else?" I suggested.

"Great idea!" Priscilla agreed.

There was a long silence while we all tried to think of something to say. Then Greta reappeared with an inscrutable expression on her face.

"How'd it go?" Helene asked.

"Fine," she replied, and skipped off, successfully avoiding any more questions.

Priscilla had slipped into the "judge's chambers" without a word, and Helene and I were left alone on the bench in the corridor. "Two down, two to go," Helene muttered.

"We weren't going to talk about it, remember?"

"I can't help it. My problem has always been that I say what's on my mind."

"Just think," I said, feigning cheerfulness, "in less than an hour, this will be a thing of the past."

"Sure. Then all we have to worry about is the results."

The trouble was, Helene zeroed in on all my fears, but I did not want to talk about them. I purposely remained silent, but that didn't matter. She went right on, babbling about percentages and how her chances were one out of four that she'd be selected, but that there was a fifty-fifty chance to be the back-up soloist. She didn't let up until Priscilla swept out, picked up her canvas bag, sighed in an offhand manner, "It was nothing," and sashayed down the hall.

Then it was my turn and I had to restrain myself from running into the music room. Mr. Saxe, looking more rumpled than ever, was sitting in a chair, and smiled at me. "Why don't you do your piece first, and then the Bach."

"Okay," I said, not trusting myself to say more without my voice cracking, and handed the sheet music that I'd been clutching to Peter. Peter played a few introductory measures and then I plunged in. This was the first time I had sung "I'll Never Walk Alone" with a full piano backup although I'd practiced at home playing with one finger. It made all the difference having an accompanist, and my nervousness disappeared almost immediately. Then I was warmed up for the Bach excerpt, and I was confident that I performed as well as I could.

When I was finished, Mr. Saxe said evenly, "Very nice. The results will be posted on the bulletin board outside this room next Monday. Now please send Helene in."

"Okay," I said, taking my music from the piano. I glanced at Peter who had remained silent as the sphinx, but I was sure he nodded his head at me almost imperceptibly and smiled with his eyes. Not exactly a wild response from him or Saxe, but at least I hadn't disgraced myself.

"Well?" Helene exclaimed, the second I came out the door.

"It's not terrible," I whispered. "Honest."

She brushed past me without saying anything and closed the door behind her. I slowly gathered up my belongings, and relived every minute of the audition. I wondered if Mr. Saxe said "very nice" automatically and if everyone received Peter's silent approval. As I ambled down the corridor, I couldn't stop smiling. I knew that was absurd because I should have been anxious about the results. Instead, all I could think about was that the tryouts were over!

2

My state of euphoria didn't last long, because as soon as I got home Daisy called and wanted to know who else had auditioned, how I did, and when I would know if I were *Numero Uno*. And that evening, my parents wouldn't have been normal if they hadn't asked me about the tryouts. After all, I'd been practicing all week. Naturally, I answered all their questions, but between them and Daisy, I found all my suppressed fears surfacing. No matter how many times I told myself it didn't matter whether I was the soloist or not, I did care. I also knew that if I didn't stay busy all weekend, by the time Monday rolled around, I would be completely unhinged.

MB seemed to sense my anxiety even though I thought I'd been deceptively calm, and suggested I help out at High Point the next day. I always enjoy working in the shop because I get paid the minimum wage and it's more fun than baby-sitting. Actually, I felt really needed because Saturday is their busiest day, and MB said that Erica had to take her kids to the dentist in the afternoon.

"If you could come in at one o'clock, you'll be saving my life," my mother pleaded.

"Sure," I said, grateful that she asked me, and thinking that helping customers select colors and patterns would take my mind off my problems.

That's exactly what happened, and I actually did get through the day without worrying about *it*. And that evening, Patsy had invited a bunch of kids over for a "make your own pasta" party. I was really looking forward to that, and when I got home from the shop, I had to get ready immediately because Daisy was going to pick me up promptly at six so that we could walk over to Patsy's house together.

It was one of those Indian summer days and I could still wear my blue and red madras cotton skirt, a white cotton Victorian blouse, and Grecian sandals. I'd just recently gotten into clothes. A year ago my best party outfit would have been my raggediest jeans and a faded blue man's shirt. I remember once taking a long time getting ready for a bash at school, and when I was finally dressed my father looked at me in alarm. "I thought you were going to a party!" he exclaimed.

"I am," I replied indignantly.

"In that?" he asked.

Before I could shout back at him—or burst into tears—MB intervened. "That's the style, dear. Leave her alone."

He just shook his head in disbelief, avoiding a scene, but now I can see what restraint he was exercising. That's probably one of the reasons he has a reputation for being such a good lawyer.

Daisy and I came to the conclusion simultaneously

that wearing a skirt, or even a dress, on occasion, wasn't retarded. "I guess it's a sign of our maturity," I said the first time we agreed to wear a skirt to school last year, just for a change. It's true, at least ten kids asked us where we were going, but gradually almost every girl in the class started wearing a skirt. That convinced us that we were leaders of fashion, and ever since, Daisy and I have uncontrollable giggling sessions thinking up what trendy clothes we might wear. Since we're both anything but far out, I don't think that will ever happen.

As I finished getting dressed for Patsy's, I thought how lucky I'd been that MB had never bugged me about clothes. I guess she knew I'd have to fight her if she did, just to prove my independence. If parents were smart, I thought, as I stared at my reflection in the mirror over the sink and carefully applied lip gloss, they'd let kids make as many decisions for themselves as possible. I was so intent on what I was doing that I wasn't aware that Daisy had arrived and been told to come upstairs, until I heard her say, "Boo!"

We'd been scaring each other like that ever since seventh grade, and I have a feeling no matter how old and sophisticated we get, we'll still be "booing." This time she really startled me.

"You look terrific. Just like I imagined," Daisy laughed. She knew what I'd be wearing without me even telling her.

"You do, too," I said, knowing she would be in her favorite summer outfit—red dirndl skirt, pink peasant blouse, and huaraches.

"Sorry I scared you," she apologized. "What were you thinking?"

"Tell you on the way over." I grabbed my bag,

hurried down the stairs with Daisy behind me, yelled goodbye to my parents, who were watching the six o'clock news in the den, and rushed out the door.

"Hey, take it easy," Daisy said, running to keep up with me. "A minute ago, you were in a trance, and now you're hyper."

"Sorry, I just have to keep moving or thinking or something."

"What are you talking about? You sound like I do before a tennis tournament."

"It's sort of the same."

"You mean the tryout, don't you? You've got to remember that there's nothing more you can do. Might as well forget about it."

"I know you're right, and I'm being ridiculous, but I can't help it."

"You were going to tell what you were thinking, remember?"

"Oh yeah," I nodded, and proceeded to elaborate on my theory about how kids and their parents were a lot better off if the parents didn't make every issue a battleground.

"I bet you're referring to the fact that your mother never got on your case about always wearing jeans."

"Exactly." I couldn't help thinking that Daisy had ESP where I was concerned.

Then we took turns listing a zillion other things that kids just naturally outgrow without their parents inter- ference.

"Messy hair," I began.

"Dirty fingernails," Daisy shot back.

"Junk food."

"Bad language."

"Taking a bath."

The list was endless, and we were so busy trying to top each other that by the time we arrived at Patsy's, I had stopped fretting—at least for the moment.

"Just in time," Patsy said, holding the door. "You're the last to arrive, but Pop has just begun to cook the ziti, fettuccine, spaghetti, tortellini, conchiglie, fusilli, and rigatoni."

"Only seven kinds of pasta," Daisy remarked, with a straight face.

"It's a small party," Patsy explained equally deadpanned, and then we all cracked up.

Patsy claims that except for a couple of bedrooms the size of closets, she lives in a one-room house. In a way, she's right, but that one room is fabulous. There's an elaborately designed kitchen at one end, a huge stone fireplace at the other, and in the middle is a living area where one could learn to drive a car.

I quickly glanced around the room and was relieved to see that there were only kids from our class, which meant I didn't have to cope with the other candidates for the solo. Not that I didn't like Pris, Helene, and Greta—I hardly knew them—but there was no way we could have avoided discussing the subject uppermost in our minds.

Patsy's father, Mr. Bocce, was wearing a chef's hat and insisted that everyone who came near him sample the sauce he was brewing. Mrs. Bocce was fixing the salad with the assistance of Tony, Patsy's ten-year-old brother. All the Bocces have dark eyes that sparkle, and an infectious enthusiasm, and treat everyone as a part of the family. It would be impossible to be in a bad mood in their house.

Mr. Bocce saw me come in and immediately called me over. "Come kiss the help," he ordered, and put down his ladle long enough to give me a bear hug. Then

Mrs. Bocce kissed me on the cheek, while Tony shoved a large green olive at me. As always, the Bocces made me feel absolutely terrific, as though I was the most important person in the room.

"Patsy tells me you're going for the soprano solo in the madrigal group," Mr. Bocce bellowed over the sound of the taped music that surrounded us.

"Going for is not the same as getting," I muttered, hoping that no one could hear our discussion.

"I betcha you win, I betcha," Tony chimed in.

"She wishes," a voice next to me hissed. I turned around just in time to see Sabrina sidle off. I knew she had a reputation for caustic remarks, but I wished she hadn't hit such an exposed nerve. I tried to pretend it didn't matter and was grateful when Evan, the head of the tenor section, asked me to dance. Daisy says Evan has had a crush on me for ages, but has the good sense to recognize that I'm not interested. I could never go for someone who hardly ever smiles. He's nice looking behind his horn-rimmed glasses, is probably the smartest person in our class, but he's off-the-wall about everything except science and music. I could just imagine kissing Evan and then having him formulate some theory about the effect of osculation on blood pressure.

I guess it was naive of me to hope that no one would mention the audition. Everyone at the party who was in the madrigal group knew about it, and naturally asked questions. Evan dismissed the whole subject by stating categorically that I had the best voice, and Saxe should overlook the fact that I was only a sophomore and choose me. I was grateful for his confidence in me, but it had a negative effect because I didn't want to get my hopes up. In order not to talk about me, I asked him what experiments he was doing. It was a safe question because Evan is always conducting experiments.

"I'm trying to determine the ill effects of nicotine on mice."

"But mice don't smoke," I remarked.

Typically, he did not see that I was making a small joke and he proceeded to explain that mice are injected with nicotine and the results are observed. All this lecturing was difficult to follow with me trying to follow his idiosyncratic dancing as well, and although I really like Evan as a friend, he seemed spacier than ever on the dance floor and I was relieved when Mike cut in.

Mike, in spite of his bulk, is amazingly graceful. However, he is not known for his tact. The first thing he said to me was, "Did you get it?"

"Get what?" I asked, playing dumb.

"The solo, what else?"

"Don't know yet, Mike," I grumbled. "And I wish everyone would stop talking about it."

"Don't start being a prima donna already."

"I'm not a prima donna," I shouted sharply.

"I didn't mean to upset you," Mike apologized. "Besides, I'd rather dance than argue."

"Me, too," I said, and tried not to be so uptight. It occurred to me that I was being as intense about the tryout as Evan was about his mice.

The rest of the evening I managed to field any questions about my future, pigged out on pasta, and generally had a terrific time. Before I went home that night, Patsy arranged to go bike riding with Daisy and me the following day. It was apple-picking time, and Patsy knew of a place where we could pick all the apples we wanted for a minimum fee. It was a perfect solution to getting me through Sunday.

Sunday night I was so exhausted from all my physical activity, that I fell asleep immediately. When I woke up Monday morning, I felt lightheaded. Whatever happened, it would be over. I couldn't wait to get to school, but I purposely made myself stall.

I timed myself so that I'd arrive at school just when the first bell rang because I didn't want to be hanging around, waiting for the doors to open. Besides, Saxe had to have time to post the notice, and I couldn't think of anything worse than hovering over a blank bulletin board which would eventually carry an announcement of my fate.

My timing was perfect, because there was the usual crush through the doors when the bell sounded just seconds after I arrived. I briskly headed up the stairs toward the music room, successfully avoiding any conversation. A couple of feet ahead of me I recognized Pris's long braid and black turtleneck. Helene passed us coming from the opposite direction. She was looking straight ahead, her eyes slightly glazed, and I don't think she saw us.

I caught up with Pris as we reached the bulletin board, took a deep breath, and read the notice. It was the simplest possible announcement.

Soloist: Beth Farley
Understudy: Greta Gordon

I had the strangest reaction, because instead of letting out a whoop of joy, which would have been normal, I had to make a superhuman effort to hold back my tears.

"At least, it's over," Pris muttered to herself. Then she turned to me. "Congratulations, Beth. That's really something for a tenth-grader."

"Thanks," I breathed, barely able to talk.

Then I noticed Greta, who was peering over my shoulder.

"Oh, I'm so excited," she whispered, her eyes wider than ever. "I can't believe it."

The second bell was clanging, which meant we had five minutes to get to our classes.

"Better move," Pris said, "and good luck to both of you."

As she rushed off, Greta looked at me and spoke softly. "There's no one I'd rather be backup for, Beth."

"Thank you, Greta. That's the nicest thing you could have said."

3

In the next few weeks I learned more about human nature than I ever had in my life. And especially about jealousy, which I had read somewhere was an emotional response of "anger, fear, and love." Being an only child, I'd never experienced the usual rivalry one has with sisters and brothers, but I found out very fast what it's like to be the target of the green-eyed monster. As Patsy put it, "a lot of noses get out of joint."

Daisy and Patsy were genuinely happy for me, and at the next madrigal rehearsal, all the kids at least politely acknowledged the fact that I was picked. Even Sabrina congratulated me, although I thought she might choke on the words.

The first clue I had that not everyone wished me well happened three weeks later. We were to start work on the Hindemith, a modern piece that had some very tricky solo parts. I had spent a lot of time studying other scores, but was late preparing for this one.

Singing is not one subject where it's possible to bluff, and my lack of preparedness was immediately obvious. Mr. Saxe had to stop and start four times, and I still messed up on the counting. Finally, he rapped his baton on the music stand and without looking at me directly, said sardonically, "This could stand a bit more wood-shedding. Let's take a five-minute break, and then back to work on the Bartok. We'll attack the Hindemith next week with all our forces."

Then he left the room, and everyone started talking at once. I really felt awful that I'd goofed so badly and slumped down in my seat, mentally kicking myself for not having worked harder. Daisy and Patsy must have known I needed cheering up because they immediately came over to where I was sitting.

"You're not supposed to know every single piece cold," Daisy assured me.

"Especially the Hindemith," Patsy added. "Besides, with modern music the audience doesn't know half the time if you've made a mistake or not."

"The soloist should know how to count." We all looked in the direction of a distinctively strident voice. It was Sabrina, who had hardly spoken to me since the tryouts. She was leaning against the wall talking to Andy, but made sure that I heard her. I felt worse than ever, but Patsy ignored her, and pulled me up by the hand. "Let's get out of here. It's really stuffy."

"Good idea," Daisy agreed, and led the way into the hall.

A bunch of kids were milling around and I couldn't help hearing Helene say, "She may have the best voice, but any of us would have known the notes by now." When she saw me, she averted her eyes, and I could see she was embarrassed.

I guess it was then I decided to never allow myself to

be put in such a vulnerable position. I hated to admit it, but they were right, and after that I always nailed down the piece before rehearsal.

It was worth it, because the next rehearsal I was able to get through the Hindemith without any fumbling, and Mr. Saxe gave me the equivalent of a rave review when I finished. "Remarkable," he announced in front of the whole group, and I noticed Peter smiling and silently clapping his hands.

When the rehearsal broke up, several kids told me how well I'd done. Even Sabrina conceded, "Quite an improvement," which I interpreted as extravagant praise.

Things settled down, more or less, after that turbulent beginning. Everyone resigned themselves to the fact that I was the soloist, and I was especially lucky that Greta was so accepting of me. Sometimes she sang solo in rehearsal, and afterward, she'd ask my opinion. Greta has a small, accurate, bell-like voice, and I could always honestly tell her she sang beautifully. She seemed to appreciate praise from me more than from anyone else in the group.

We rehearsed once a week through the rest of the school year, and of course there were plenty of snags, but we could feel ourselves becoming a cohesive group. Saxe had a temper tantrum periodically, usually if some of us didn't know our notes and had to spend time in sectional rehearsals learning them, or if we were late. That drove him crazy. But all the rough edges of our singing were smoothed down, and most of the emotional outbursts were kept to a minimum.

It wasn't until that final week of rehearsal that I again felt people's antagonism toward me, and all because I defended Mr. Saxe's demanding schedule. I was tired, too, and like everyone else, felt I'd run a twenty-six mile marathon by the time we boarded the bus for the airport.

Early on, there was a small crisis about who would chaperone us on the trip. We all had hoped it would be Mrs. Saxe, who we'd met at a number of school events. She was the logical choice, because she was warm, friendly, motherly, and Mr. Saxe obviously adored her. But unfortunately, she was unable to take time off from her job as a social worker at the "Y" where she was setting up a summer program. When Mr. Saxe told us, he looked as forlorn as a puppy, but then he promised us we wouldn't be disappointed with whomever was chosen. The decision was to be made by him and the principal of the school, Mr. Carlo.

After days of speculation, Saxe announced that the physical education teacher, Julie Green, and her husband, Clyde, would accompany us. We all let out a roar of approval because Julie, who looks like a teen-ager herself—small, wiry, energetic—even though she's at least thirty, is "with it," and yet has a quiet air of authority. We never met her husband until the day of departure, and he was the source of constant speculation. Mr. Saxe had told us he was a poet who taught English at a local college. As was to be expected, we outdid ourselves based on this skimpy information, conjuring up images of what he was like. The final picture we concocted was of a pale Woody Allen, without Woody's sense of humor, an ivory-tower type who was probably terrified at the prospect of herding a team of teen-agers around an alien land more than three thousand miles from home.

As it turned out, Clyde was at least a head taller than Julie, looked more like an athlete than a poet, except for a neatly trimmed Vandyke, and was totally at ease in handling what he later poetically described as a "rash of raging hormones." What Mr. Saxe had failed to tell us was that Clyde also coached the swimming team at the college where he was a teacher. "Ivory-tower type" was the most inaccurate description imaginable!

It was "all systems go" on D-day, the Sunday we would depart. Everything had been anticipated, including the detail that involved putting red wool balls on our luggage so that it could be easily identified. We were allowed one suitcase each, which Mr. Saxe said we should be capable of carrying at least 100 feet without excessive breathing.

We met at four o'clock in the afternoon at school where the bus that would take us to the airport awaited us. Everyone was on time, even Flos, who had gained the reputation of being the ultimate space case. Flos is pretty, dark-haired, and dimpled, and she blended perfectly in the choir. But she couldn't be trusted to follow instructions in anything except music.

We couldn't wait to get started and avoided any prolonged farewells with our parents, some of whom were embarrassingly teary considering our advanced age. Then we were introduced to Clyde, who handed us our tickets after we showed him our passports, and piled onto the bus. The line had been moving steadily, when suddenly it stopped. Flos was fumbling in her bag, and then, looking panicked, cried out, "Oh no, I forgot it!"

Her mother and father had been watching and immediately began yelling at each other.

"I know she's going to get lost over there. We never should have let her go!" her prim-looking mother shouted.

"It was your idea, remember. You thought it might help her mature." Her father's voice was as stern as his looks.

At first we had thought the situation was hilarious, but as Flos's parents' voices rose angrily, our laughter subsided. Flos, crimson with embarrassment, backed out of the bus, muttering, "I know I left it on my dresser. What'll I do?"

"No problem," Clyde reassured her. "The reason we've started so early is to allow time for such a possibility."

Mr. Saxe, who was standing with his wife apart from the group, gave Clyde an "I-told-you-so" look, and immediately turned back to his wife. Meanwhile, Flos shuffled toward her parents, her head bent. "I'm sorry," she mumbled. "I purposely left it out so I wouldn't forget it. I'll run home and be back in less than ten minutes."

"You'll do nothing of the kind," her father snapped. "You might just stop off for a soda, and miss the plane. Where do you think you left your passport?"

"It's on my dresser. I know that for sure."

"You stay here with your mother. I'll get it, and I think I should bring back a leash as well." He chuckled at his dark humor as he strode off.

"You think it's on your dresser," Flos's mother said. "Maybe it's on your desk, or perhaps in the bathroom. Who knows, with you? I better help him look." With that, she hurried after her husband.

Everyone was relieved that the "scene" was over, and resumed their manic mood. By the time Flos's parents returned, her father triumphantly waving the passport, we were all on the bus singing a Beatles song at the top of our lungs. I don't know if it was intentional or not, but the noise we created successfully protected Flos from any more public scolding. Julie made a final head count, and we were set to go.

When the bus driver revved up the motor, we all

scrambled to one side and frantically waved to our parents until they were out of sight. An outsider would have thought we were being shipped off into space. Then we settled, in a manner of speaking, into our seats. Clyde stood at the head of the bus, held up his hands to get our attention, congratulated us for completing the first leg of the trip successfully—a remark that was received with animal-house shrieks—and warned us that the hard part was about to come. "We have to check in at the Pan Am counter, suitcases in hand, as soon as we arrive. Then we'll have about an hour before meeting at our departure gate."

"What'll we do for an hour?" Kiki piped up. Kiki, the youngest and smallest member of the group, will probably never outgrow her role of "baby."

"You'll think pleasant thoughts," Clyde answered, and he went right on with his instructions. "In order to avoid personal loss, meaning the loss of a person, we'll have the buddy system. Whomever you are sitting next to right now will be your buddy. Don't go anywhere without your buddy!"

"What if he's a boy and I have to go you-know-where?" Kiki asked innocently.

While the rest of us laughed hysterically, Clyde shrugged his shoulders in despair. "I'll see you at the airport," he finished, and sat down.

The next phase of the operation was completed with a minimum of mishaps. Everyone managed to hang onto his or her suitcase until it was checked through. Then our seats were assigned and we hung around until it was time to meet at the departure gate. Sabrina was the only one of us who was stopped by the radar check. The metal object she was carrying in her handbag was not a suspected deadly weapon but a curling iron.

Julie made a final head count—even Flos had found

the correct gate—and then the flight attendant announced that we could board. We restrained ourselves from trampling the other passengers, found our seats, and fastened our seat belts. Before we knew it, our 747 was taxiing down the runway. Our adventure was about to begin.

When we landed at Heathrow Airport, we were bedraggled and bleary-eyed from lack of sleep and nervous anticipation. We managed to get through passport control without incident and then meet at the baggage claim counter. The group was still buzzing with excitement while waiting for our luggage when an exceptionally handsome young Englishman dashed through the gates marked NO ENTRY—obviously he had connections. He immediately approached Mr. Saxe, greeted him profusely, and then shook hands with Julie and Clyde. We were relatively quiet as we watched the ritual, and then Mr. Saxe said, "This is Tom Savage, our courier."

"Our courier," Patsy whispered in my ear, "wow!"

She expressed my feelings precisely, and I tried to recall what Mr. Saxe had told us about couriers when he had first talked about the tour. He had mentioned that we would be assigned someone who would take care of our lodgings, rehearsal and concert schedules, transportation, eating arrangements, and even our sight-seeing expeditions and free time. Saxe didn't know at that time if the courier would be male or female, but Education in England (EIE), the organization that had orchestrated the tour, guaranteed him that the courier would handle all the nitty-gritty details.

"Tom will be taking care of us for the next twenty-one days," Mr. Saxe continued, "and now he'd just like to say hello."

"Greetings, choir," Tom began, in the most educated and resonant voice. "As soon as our luggage comes through, and each one of you can identify your valise, I'll arrange for it to be transported to the hotel, and you can follow me to the bus."

"I'd follow him anywhere," Sabrina murmured.

Me, too, I thought to myself, as I took in his extraordinary features—thick chestnut-colored wavy hair, dark blue penetrating eyes, and a ruddy complexion. He was tall, at least six feet two, and hardly skinny, but he moved with enormous ease.

"The Prince Edward Hotel, where we will be staying, is about a thirty-minute bus ride. I'll give you your room assignments once we board the bus." We had agreed on roommates before we left the States, and Daisy and I had paired off. We joked about having twenty enforced sleepovers.

Tom went on about getting settled in our rooms, taking it easy because of jet lag, meeting in the dining room of the hotel for lunch at noon, and being prepared for further briefing.

"I hate to be a bore, choir, but it's my job to provide you with information and keep everyone on schedule."

You, boring? Never! It was fortunate no one could read my mind because I didn't want to appear foolish. Besides, I didn't believe in love at first sight. However, I was mesmerized by Tom's looks, as well as his voice, and it wasn't until I felt Daisy tugging on my arm that I could stop staring at him, even as he moved off.

"Hey, Beth, it's time to move," she urged.

"Huh?" I mumbled.

"Move," she repeated. "Our suitcases have been loaded on the luggage cart and we're supposed to head for the bus."

"Did mine get on?" I asked. "I forgot to notice."

"I noticed you forgot to notice," Daisy chuckled, "but I checked it out for you."

"Oh, thanks. I guess I was dreaming."

"You might call it that," Daisy said with a knowing smile.

Once we climbed into the bus, which was equipped with a microphone, Tom took over completely. He gave us our room assignments, commented on the super highway, charmingly apologized for the uninteresting scenery, said he knew we were exhausted and promised not to tax us further with information until we had had lunch. Finally, he welcomed us to England and assured us that his role for the next three weeks was to make us happy.

We applauded vigorously as he sat down, and I personally thought that just knowing he was around would make me happy. I was sure he had a zillion girls pursuing him, and he wouldn't look at me. And although I've never been especially shy around boys, maybe that was because I'd never been that interested. I wondered how I would react if he did pay attention to me: cool and sophisticated, coy, or awkward. These thoughts occupied me for the entire bus trip. I was grateful that everyone had quieted down. Most of the group had brought tape recorders with earphones, and listened to their own music whenever possible, such as now. The others were nodding off, including Daisy.

It wasn't until Daisy and I were getting settled in our room at the Prince Edward—a small, modest, but sparkling clean hotel—that Daisy the clairvoyant intruded on my thoughts. "I think every girl here must feel the way you do," she began.

"How do I feel?"

"That Tom's really cute."

"And charming."

"And probably phony."

"Why do you say that?" It wasn't easy for me not to sound annoyed.

"Just a hunch."

"That's not fair. You can't form a judgment about someone you've only known a couple of hours."

"You're right, Beth. We didn't come here to discuss the merits of our courier, and besides, it's time for us to go downstairs. I'm anxious to check out that famous English beef-and-kidney pie, and trifle."

"Me, too," I lied. The last thing I was interested in was food. The only thing I wanted to check out was Tom Savage, whose image personified the consummate *beau garçon*.

Since we were on the third floor, we decided to walk down the stairs. Once we arrived on the main floor, we had to cross in front of the "lift" to reach the dining room. Daisy, who was several steps ahead of me, was already in the dining room when I had my first physical contact with Tom. We collided as he was rushing out of the lift and practically knocked me over. My reaction was the same as if I'd received an electrical shock.

"So sorry," he exclaimed, putting his hands on my shoulders. "Are you all right?"

"Not sure," I gasped, hoping he'd see the necessity of keeping his hands on me. He towered over me, and as I looked up into his navy blue eyes, I definitely felt weak.

His hands slid slowly down my arms, and then he held me by the wrists, as though to make sure I was steady on my feet. "We've got to stop meeting like this," he joked, "but it's not a bad way of getting to know someone in a hurry. Incidentally, what's your name?"

"Beth Farley."

"Beth Farley," he repeated. "What a lovely name."

"You really think so?"

"Yes, it's lovely, it suits you."

I had been so enthralled with our brief encounter that I had blotted out the fact that we were in a hotel lobby. Then a familiar voice called, "Tom, I'm saving a seat for you, remember?" It was Sabrina, and I couldn't believe she had made her move so fast.

"Beth, I've got to go," Tom said, gently letting go of my wrists, "but our meeting will be permanently etched in my mind."

"I'll never forget it," I murmured, holding him with my eyes as he backed off. The problem was, he undoubtedly thought I was kidding, but I'd never been more serious in my life.

I purposely waited until Tom was well ahead of me because I didn't want Sabrina, or anyone else, to get the idea that I was hanging onto him. Then I ambled into the dining room where almost all the seats were taken at the small tables that accommodated only four people. Daisy spotted me and indicated that she had saved a place.

"What happened to you?" she asked. "Did you get lost?"

"In a way," I replied mysteriously. Peter and Evan were at our table and I certainly didn't want to elaborate on my episode with Tom.

"You do look a little shaky," Peter observed perceptively. "Are you sure you're okay?"

"I'm fine," I insisted.

"It takes a while to acclimate to a new environment, different air and water," Evan pontificated.

And different boys, I thought silently. Then, before I was forced to make any further explanation, we were indeed served a beef-and-kidney pie, which took the attention off me. I tried to concentrate on my food, but I couldn't avoid seeing Tom. He was two tables away, but directly in my line of vision. I noticed that Sabrina was giving him the full treatment, resting her hand on his arm while she talked to him in animated fashion. I wondered if Tom told Sabrina she had a lovely name that suited her, or was that a spontaneous remark meant only for me? Perhaps he had another memorable line for her.

Daisy had mentioned something about English women having beautiful complexions, and that started Evan on a discourse regarding the beneficial effects of English climate on pores. He droned on, oblivious to whether or not we were listening, and I became so absorbed in wondering about Tom that I put down my fork.

"You don't like this," Peter commented, pointing to my plate.

"I'm just not hungry, I guess."

"Have to keep your strength up you know." Then he lowered his voice so only I could hear. "You're the mainstay of the group."

"Me?" I asked, nonplussed.

"As far as I'm concerned, you are."

"Thank you, Peter. Coming from you, that's really a compliment."

He smiled shyly, and a faint blush colored his face. Neither of us knew what to say next, but then Tom stood up, asked for our attention, and proceeded to tell us the program for the rest of the day.

"One hour after lunch, at precisely 2:30, we will meet on the second floor, suite 202, which is equipped with a piano, for rehearsal. This evening will be free, you'll be given a dinner allowance, but I suggest you retire no later than 10:30. Julie will pass out our day-to-day schedules, as well as a brochure that describes the English currency. Now, don't forget, room 202, with your music, of course. I personally can't wait to hear you sing. I've been told I'll be knocked out of my socks!"

"What's happened to British understatement?" Mr. Saxe growled from the corner of the room where he'd been sitting.

"You're right, Mr. Saxe. I should have said that as high-school choirs go, I hear you're almost acceptable." This was greeted with disapproving whistles, and Tom, blocking his view of Mr. Saxe with his hand, added quickly, "But I still can't wait to hear you." Then he promptly sat down, and there was scattered applause.

"He can even handle Mr. Saxe," I remarked.

"Yeah," Peter agreed, without enthusiasm.

"A natural politician," Evan observed.

"That's what he is," Daisy said sarcastically.

Again, I sensed that Daisy wasn't enamored of Tom, and more understandably, neither were Peter or Evan. Still, I thought he was adorable, and I believed him when he said he couldn't wait to hear us sing. Perhaps I bent over backward to think he was telling the truth, because I couldn't wait to sing for him.

4

Suite 202 easily accommodated the madrigal group and the audience, which consisted of Julie, Clyde, and Tom, who seated themselves at the far end of the room. The first thing Mr. Saxe had us do was our massage and zoo routine. Massage meant we formed two lines and took turns rubbing each other's back. I'm not sure what good it did for our vertebrae, but it did a lot for our spirits. After ten minutes of that, we were led through a series of animal noises, with Mr. Saxe acting out the various roles of gorilla, pig, cow, and elephant. We never agreed on the exact sound of an elephant, but settled on something between a grunt and a bellow, which had us in hysterics. By the time these preliminaries were over, we were definitely warmed up.

Next, we ran through our scales and finally started work on our repertoire. We sang several madrigals straight through without Saxe's usual starts and stops, and when we were finished Julie, Clyde, and Tom applauded wildly. Saxe turned to them and bowed stiffly, and then proceeded to demand his customary perfection.

The rehearsal was arduous and lasted almost two hours, but it didn't seem that long to me. We had been trained, upon penalty of death, to focus on our conductor, but whenever possible I glanced at Tom. We didn't work on any of my arias, but I did have a small solo in one of the madrigals. When I was finished, I looked for Tom's reaction, but nothing registered on his face. Was it possible he didn't notice me singing alone? Was I expecting too much? Was it my imagination, or did he only have eyes for Sabrina? I tried not to dwell on that possibility, and forced myself to pay attention to Mr. Saxe.

When rehearsal was over, Tom stood up and thanked us. "In deference to Mr. Saxe, I can only say you're not half bad."

"Translated into American English, that means you're terrific," Clyde explained.

"You're so good," Julie added, "that I'm going to pass out your supper allowance and a list of restaurants. You can go off by yourselves, if you wish, but Tom will be escorting a group to Bumbles, and Clyde and I are going to Kebab and Houmus."

Everyone started talking at once, and Daisy, Patsy and I found ourselves together. "I vote for Kebab and Houmus," Patsy exclaimed. "I love Greek food."

"Me, too," said Daisy. "There's nothing like a stuffed grape leaf."

"Bumbles sounds so typically English. I think I'll try that," I remarked as casually as possible.

If Daisy knew my real reason for choosing Bumbles, she was tactful enough not to say anything.

As it turned out, we were divided almost equally into three separate groups. Mine, surprisingly, did not include Sabrina. Perhaps I had exaggerated her interest in Tom. However, the fact that she wasn't with us didn't mean I had Tom to myself. Kiki, Priscilla, Flos, and Helene were with us, Mike was the only other boy, and all the girls were vying for Tom's attention. It was good in one way, because the girls, Kiki especially, asked him a zillion questions that I wanted to know the answers to.

As soon as we were seated at a round table, Kiki began.

"How old are you?" was her first question.

"Nineteen."

"I suppose you're at Oxford or Cambridge."

"Cambridge, couldn't you tell?"

"A freshman?"

"Just completed my first year."

The waiter was passing out menus and Tom interrupted the inquisition long enough to help us determine what to order. There were a couple of French dishes on the menu, and he pronounced them impeccably.

"You must be majoring in French," Helene said.

"No, but I am fluent in the language, as well as in Italian and German."

"Wow," Flos muttered. "I could barely get through Spanish I."

"Me, too," Mike laughed.

"It's easier for the English," Pris interjected. "They're exposed to foreign languages much earlier, and they're so much closer to the other countries."

"You're right about that," Tom conceded. "But before we get into a discussion of the differences between American and English education, I think we should order."

"Right, sir," said the waiter who had been standing patiently by our table.

Then Tom smoothly took over, asking everyone what they wanted. Tom explained to Kiki, who had requested a hamburger and French fries, that "this was not the place," and he told the waiter who had offered him a wine list that Perrier would be sufficient *"pour les enfants."*

As soon as the waiter left with our order, the girls continued to quiz Tom. I didn't want to ask a lot of questions, but I did want Tom to notice me, and finally I had an opportunity.

"What are you majoring in, if not languages?" Helene asked.

"I'm reading law."

"Reading—what's that mean?"

"It means that the three years I'm at Cambridge, all my studies are concentrated in one area. At the end of that time, I will pass my exams, presumably with all firsts, and become a barrister with one of the more prestigious English law firms."

This may have sounded arrogant, but he spoke so matter-of-factly it didn't seem to me that he was bragging.

"My father's a lawyer," I said, the first contribution I'd made to the discussion.

"Your father's a lawyer," Tom repeated with surprising interest. "Lucky I didn't do any serious damage to you outside the lift, Beth. You might have sued." He winked at me knowingly, and I relished the idea that we had our own private joke.

"What kind of barrister do you want to be?" Pris asked, ignoring the byplay between Tom and me.

"International law," he told her. Then he singled me out again. "Beth, what does your father specialize in?"

"General practice. He does a lot of trial work."

"Wonderful," Tom muttered.

Why does he think that's so wonderful? I wondered.

"My father's a doctor," Helene said. She was probably hoping for a similar reaction from Tom, but he simply nodded his head politely in her direction.

"A neurologist," she added, and looked at him expectantly.

"That's nice." His response was indifferent, and then he turned back to me. "Is your father with a large firm?"

"Medium-sized."

"I suppose he's a partner."

"Yes, just last year he was made one."

"Hey, you sound like you're looking for a job," Mike observed.

Tom didn't answer, just chuckled, and then dropped the subject completely. By the time we had finished our "pudd," Tom had included everyone in the conversation. We discussed everything from how the English raise their children—much stricter than American parents—to the pros and cons of being sent to a boarding school at the age of eight.

"The English independent school, which you colonists call a private school in the States, and which we call public, is much more demanding. Our school vacations in the summer are just over a month, there's no messing around with gut courses, and we're deadly serious about preparing for our A-levels, which determine whether we'll get into university."

Of course we defended the "colonists" and expressed our shock that eight year olds would be sent away from home to be educated, but Tom deftly countered our arguments without losing his cool. It was seven against one, after all, but he didn't seem to mind being on the firing line.

When it came time for the bill, Tom brought out his pencil-thin calculator and rapidly figured out to the last cent what each of us owed. "This includes the v.a.t.— value added tax—and also the tip. You can pay me later," he told us, taking out his wallet and discreetly leaving the correct amount under the bill on the plate that the waiter had presented.

One of the idioms I'd learned in French was *savoir-faire*, which means the ability to say and do the right thing in any situation. That was Tom, personified. I couldn't imagine him ever making a false step. I even admired the way he dressed, something I never particularly thought about when it came to boys. Occasionally, I noticed Evan's hotdog combinations—a mustard-colored sweater over a sausage-pink shirt—but generally I was indifferent to what boys wore. However, Tom's clothes were something else. He wore a black turtleneck, a brown tweed jacket with suede patches on the elbows, tapered beige trousers, and buttery soft polished loafers.

"It's only nine o'clock," Tom said when we got outside the restaurant. "How about a stroll over to Piccadilly Circus?"

"I love the circus!" Kiki shouted.

"This is different," Tom said patiently, while the rest of us looked at each other and groaned.

"Only kidding," Kiki sighed, but it was hard to tell whether or not she really did expect to see acrobats, clowns, and prancing horses.

The rest of us agreed that we'd love to go and Tom assumed his role as guide, providing us with fascinating bits of information as we ambled along.

"Did you know where Piccadilly got its name?" he asked.

"Sounds like some kind of candy," Flos answered.

"Or herb," Pris offered.

"Good guesses, but you're off the mark. The story goes that in 1612 on the corner of Piccadilly, there was a very popular shop run by a tailor who specialized in selling pickadils, or lace collars. Supposedly, this famous thoroughfare was named after these collars."

"You're certainly well informed," Helene complimented.

"Yeah, how come you know so much?" Mike teased.

"It's in the courier's handbook that we should have all such bits and bobs of information at our fingertips."

"Wow," Flos uttered for the hundredth time that night. Then, in her usual spacey way, she didn't stop at the crosswalk we had come to and proceeded to cross the street. If Tom hadn't lunged after her and pulled her back onto the curb, she would have been sideswiped by a car that was turning from the opposite lane. We gasped in horror when we realized how close she had come to being hit.

"That's an excellent way to damage yourself," Tom remarked evenly, still holding onto her arm.

"I think you saved my life," Flos, looking ashen, muttered.

"It says in the courier handbook to avoid losing our clients, especially from vehicular accidents."

His treating the matter lightly relieved the tension, and we could actually smile when he suggested that two people be assigned to Flos for the rest of the night walk. "Not only to protect Flos, but to save me from cardiac arrest."

"I'll take care of Flos by myself," Mike volunteered, putting her arm in his.

She looked at him warmly, and murmured, "I know you will, Mike."

There was some tittering from the others at this open display of affection—none of us had thought of Mike and Flos as an item—but I couldn't laugh at anyone's romance.

When we approached Piccadilly Circus, the atmosphere dramatically changed. It was noisy, exciting, teeming with characters, and a little bit scary. Tom described the statue, the Angel of Christian Charity, that stands in the center of the plaza surrounded by a fountain.

"It was designed in 1893 in honor of the Victorian philanthropist Lord Shaftesbury."

I had gravitated to Tom's side and was hanging on to every word. "It looks like Eros, the god of love," I pointed out.

"A lot of people think that, because of the bow and arrow, but actually, they're a play on Shaftesbury's name."

Just then a couple of rowdies, who had probably had too much to drink, brushed by me so closely that in order to avoid being pushed over I literally fell against Tom, who caught me in his arms.

"Be careful," he cautioned, helping me get my balance and turning me around to face him.

I was aware that he was still holding me unnecessarily close. "I keep bumping into you," I said idiotically.

"I don't mind, Beth. I want to take care of you."

I tried desperately to think of something to say when Kiki came bounding over to us, apparently oblivious to our romantic clinch, and shouted, "Clyde and Julie and a whole bunch of kids from our group are here."

"That's nice," Tom remarked, without taking his

eyes off me. Then he slowly released me and I felt very light-headed, but I knew it wasn't from my near collision with the rowdies. It was because I was in London on a perfect summer night with Tom Savage, who had just said, "I want to take care of you."

I was reminded of Wordsworth's line, which had more to do with the French Revolution than it did with love in Piccadilly: "Bliss was it in that dawn to be alive,/But to be young was very heaven."

The next day there was practically no free time. In the morning we had an intensive three-hour rehearsal, at noon a less-than-leisurely lunch, in the afternoon more rehearsal, and then we had to get ready for our first English concert. It was to take place at four o'clock at a boys' school. Saxe referred to it as our English debut and warned us not to be late boarding the bus.

"Three o'clock, prompt. If you're late, we'll leave without you," he threatened, and we knew him too well not to take him seriously.

I hadn't spoken to Tom since the previous night. He was busy with arrangements, and only ducked into the rehearsal room briefly. In a way I was pleased because I had to rehearse a couple of Schubert songs and I wanted to surprise Tom with my solo. At lunch, he sat with Mr. Saxe, Clyde and Julie, probably figuring out logistics.

When the afternoon rehearsal was over, we only had a half hour to change into our concert garb, white blouses and long black skirts for the girls, navy blue blazers and dark gray slacks for the boys. The minute we were dismissed, Daisy and I bolted up the stairs to our room and scurried around getting ready. We had to share a community bathroom down the hall, but there was a sink in our room where we could wash up.

Daisy was bent over the sink, splashing water over her face, when she suddenly sputtered, "You're lucky you're not in love."

"Why?" I asked. I wanted to stick to my resolve not to talk about Tom even though I had fallen asleep reliving every minute that we'd spent together, and all day I could barely get through an hour without thinking about him.

"Well, I'm having a great time here, but I really miss Greg."

"I can understand that," I sympathized.

Then, she surprised me by asking, "How did you make out with blue eyes last night?"

"You mean Tom?"

"Who else?"

"He happens to be very nice, and very sophisticated." I thought that was a neutral statement.

"I never thought 'sophisticated' was your type." She was blotting her face with a towel but I could see her eyes had a mischievous look, and I stopped being defensive.

"Neither did I," I agreed, and we both giggled.

Daisy had finished washing, and then I took over the sink. As I buried my face in a washcloth, I was relieved that Daisy didn't ask any more questions about Tom. This was the first time I didn't want to share my innermost feelings with her, and I wasn't sure why. Was it because I was growing up and didn't have to tell everything? Was it because I still sensed her disapproval, or was it because I wasn't that sure of him myself? Probably a bit of all three.

We were almost finished dressing when Patsy burst into our room.

"Ten minutes 'til countdown. Are you ready?"

"Two secs," Daisy said, stuffing a sweater into her canvas bag.

"Oh no," I yelped, as I tried to fasten my skirt. "My button just popped. Do you have a safety pin?"

"Better than that. My mother, who thinks of everything, insisted I bring a traveling sewing kit. I'll go get it." Patsy disappeared while I grumbled about bad timing, but I had just pulled off my skirt when she rushed in, sewing kit in hand.

"You're a lifesaver," I said, taking the kit from her. Then I made three unsuccessful attempts to thread the needle.

"Here, let me do that," Daisy demanded, grabbing the needle and thread, and deftly performing what I was finding an insurmountable task.

"What would I do without you two?" I asked.

"You'd be known as the skirtless soprano," Patsy joked.

"Be great for the Bryant School reputation," Daisy piped up.

We were warming up to one of our giggling fits, so I warned them they'd better get going without me. "I can sew a button on a lot faster all by myself. There's no point in three of us cutting it so close."

"You're right. Remember, though, you've got exactly six minutes," Daisy cautioned.

"Okay, okay. I'll be there," I promised. I had already begun sewing as they left the room, and it didn't take me more than several minutes to pull on my skirt, tuck in my blouse, collect my music, grab a sweater and my bag, and leave.

The hall was deserted and I knew I'd be the last one ready for the bus. I ran all the way downstairs, ungracefully holding my skirt as I leapt down the last two steps.

Then, to my astonishment, I saw Tom and Sabrina. They were at the side of the stairwell, their heads almost touching, deep in conversation.

"Hi, Beth," Tom greeted me. For the first time, he seemed flustered and I wasn't about to make things easier for him, so I remained silent.

"Tom's been trying to explain the British monetary system to me," Sabrina said. "I just can't seem to get it into my head."

"That's right," Tom said, a little too quickly.

Sure, I thought, it's really necessary to hide out under a stairwell, almost kissing each other, in order to understand English money.

I whisked out of the hotel and heard Tom call after me, "Hold the bus, Beth. It's bad form for the courier to be late." Obviously, he'd recovered from his momentary embarrassment.

There were many unoccupied seats and I chose one near a window at the back of the bus. I dumped my things on the empty seat next to me and stared out the window. Everyone was jabbering excitedly and no one noticed that I wasn't participating.

Tom, who always sat at the front of the bus near the microphone, was telling us that once we arrived at the boys' school we would leave our belongings in a room behind the auditorium where we would have a fifteen-minute warm-up; after the concert there would be a reception and high tea; and then the bus would take us to Westminster Bridge where we would embark on a night cruise up the Thames. After that announcement, there were deafening cheers and I found myself caught up in the excitement. What could be more romantic than a night cruise on the Thames!

But then my somber mood returned, for what's so great about a romantic atmosphere if there's no one to share it with? I'd always prided myself on my ability to talk myself in and out of things, and on my willpower. I was just going to have to use those attributes to talk myself out of flipping for Tom. For starters, I tried hard to think of his faults, but I drew a blank. Maybe when I got to know him better I'd see some flaw that I could exaggerate, make it dominate my thinking about him, and then I would no longer regard him as perfect. Also, I had my singing to think about and the last thing I wanted was to have my infatuation with a Cambridge man, who I'd probably never see again after these three weeks, to interfere with my performance. The other factor I had to face was that Tom might have an English girlfriend, and he was just being nice to me in the line of duty.

I figured that if I persisted in thinking up reasons not to get involved with Tom, I'd be in control of the situation. I had always made fun of self-help books that preach the power of positive thinking—or negative thinking, if necessary—but if that philosophy worked, why not. Anything would be better than suffering an unrequited love.

I was so absorbed in these thoughts as I gazed out the window that I was unaware of someone putting my things on the floor and then slumping into the seat next to me.

"How you doing?" an unmistakably sonorous voice asked.

"Me?" I responded stupidly, turning to face the object of my musings.

"That's who I care about," Tom murmured, and gave me a half-smile that made me, as well as my carefully thought-out resolutions, melt. Then his hand surreptitiously reached for mine, and he squeezed it meaningfully.

I struggled futilely to remember my plan to put Tom in proper perspective, but my heart was beating too fast, and seemingly of its own volition, my hand squeezed his back. Then, knowing we shouldn't be seen like this, we reluctantly let go.

"Sometimes," Tom spoke softly, "it's not easy to be a courier."

"What do you mean? It looks great to me."

"In some ways, yes. But I have to spread myself too thin. Be available to everyone, answer a lot of zany questions, not show any favoritism."

"You mean you can't always be with the person you'd like to be with."

"What do you think?"

I watched him stand up and then carefully pick up my things and return them to the seat. "You can't stay here?" I couldn't help but sound plaintive.

"Wish I could, but the courier's handbook says . . ."

"You don't have to explain," I interrupted.

He leaned over and muttered confidentially, "The problems of being a courier." Then he slowly made his way down the aisle, making remarks to everyone along the way. Was I crazy, or did he purposely avoid stopping at Sabrina's row? She was on the aisle, and he must have seen her. Was it a conspicuous snub for the benefit of the rest of us, especially me? Was I reading too much into everything Tom said or did?

I was distracted from these speculations when the bus slowed, and turned into a tree-lined drive. Somehow we had arrived in the outskirts of London without me hardly noticing, and I was surprised to suddenly see so much greenery.

"Look to the right," Tom was saying over the microphone, "and you can glimpse St. George's cricket field. There's no one playing now, but quite honestly, for Americans our traditional summer game is not much more interesting when there are players on the field."

Everyone chuckled at his making fun of his country's pastime, and all my good feelings about Tom were reinforced. The more I saw Tom in action, the more I was attracted to him. When, if ever, would I find the flaw?

There was a group of unobtrusively gray buildings speckling the landscape and the driver pulled up to one of them and opened the door of the bus. Mr. Saxe and Tom were the first ones off the bus, and immediately a faculty member wearing a houndstooth jacket burst out of the building and greeted them effusively. As the rest of us filed off the bus, Tom informally introduced us to Mr. Robinson, whose mellifluous tones belied his rather disheveled appearance.

We followed Mr. Robinson into the building, efficiently decorated with contemporary furniture, and he kept up a non-stop patter about how St. George's had been transplanted from the inner city of London to the vastly superior spacious suburbs.

"The boys have adapted exceedingly well to these modern facilities. Quite a departure from the old St. George's which was all furbelows and fretwork. I rather like the simplicity of the new architecture myself."

He rattled on until we'd arrived at what he referred to as the "preparatory" room and then he addressed us formally: "As head of the music department, it is my privilege to extend to you, on behalf of the St. George's School for Boys, greetings and salutations. We have looked forward to your visit eagerly and wish you a most successful tour. Don't forget, we are laying on a high tea in the hall just east of the auditorium. Good luck, choir."

By the time he left, we were like a pack of racehorses at the starting gate, but Mr. Saxe calmed us down. He remained incredibly cool, instilling us all with confidence, and he assured us we would do credit to ourselves, to Bryant High School, and especially to the choir ensemble. Then he had us run through some tough spots in the Italian madrigals that had given us trouble, and finally it was time for the concert.

We took our places on the stage while the audience politely applauded. Mr. Saxe strode to the podium, bowed, and then thanked St. George's for its hospitality.

"We couldn't have a better place to begin our tour of England." With that, the audience, which had seemed unusually restrained considering it consisted of schoolboys, showed its approval by an outbreak of loud clapping. Mr. Saxe was forced to interrupt, suggesting that the enthusiasm be saved for the performance, and then he announced the program. I was totally unprepared when he announced, "Our accompanist is Peter Howell and our soprano soloist is Beth Farley."

Hearing my name singled out before a humungus audience unnerved me, and I wondered if Peter felt the same way. If he did, he didn't show it, and as he played an introduction to our first set of Hungarian madrigals, he seemed totally secure. Just watching him helped me to relax.

The program had been planned without an intermission and my Schubert solo was the next to last piece. I'm not sure how I survived until then, but I remembered how desperately I'd wanted to be chosen and now that I had my opportunity to perform, I just couldn't blow it. If I thought the tryouts were nerveracking, this was even worse. If I didn't do credit to myself, to Bryant High School, and to the choir, as Mr. Saxe had guaranteed, I think I'd fold up and die. What if my voice cracked, or I had a memory lapse?

Then it was time for me to step forward. As Mr. Saxe cued Peter, I hoped I didn't look as scared as I felt. I knew the score by heart and therefore didn't have to hold the music in front of me. That was fortunate because I'm sure I could not have stopped my hands from shaking.

Now that I was close to the edge of the stage, I could see the audience clearly. It was packed with boys who wore maroon-colored jackets with a St. George's emblem on the pocket. They were mostly all teen-agers, although some might have been as young as twelve. I had heard the expression "a swimming sea of faces," and now I knew what it meant. I had one ridiculous thought just before Mr. Saxe indicated with his baton that I should begin: thank goodness my button had popped earlier!

Then I clasped my hands in front of me and I started to sing. The words were in German but I had studied the translation so that I knew their meaning perfectly. Mr. Saxe had taught me that I should concentrate on the sense of the song, so that even though my listeners did not know the language, they would glean the feeling of the music. It was a song about love and nothing could have been more appropriate to my mood. I really did get into it and when I finished there was a wave of applause and Mr. Saxe nodded approvingly. I glanced at Peter, whose musical opinion I trusted completely. He was all smiles and unobtrusively held up two fingers in a v for victory sign. As I floated back to my place in the soprano section, I was on cloud nine. Our last piece on the program was "The New

Jerusalem," a stirring English anthem that the audience loved.

I never felt so heady. I knew I'd sung well, I was beginning to think my feelings for Tom were reciprocated, and there were still nineteen days left of what I was sure would be the best time of my life.

5

We were all slightly manic after the concert, bubbling over with undisguised self-satisfaction as we pulled ourselves together in the preparatory room. Only Sandy, a tall, gangly ninth grader who was one of the youngest in the group, was out of it. She was in the corner, facing the wall, and her shoulders were heaving.

Everyone was rushing around getting ready to go to the reception and didn't seem to notice her. I quietly walked over to where she was standing and asked her what was wrong.

She calmed down long enough to look at me sideways and replied, "Nothing."

"Then why are you crying?" I persisted.

"Because I'm so happy," she explained, with a fresh outburst of weeping.

I was really bewildered and didn't know what to do,

when Peter came over to us and looked at me questioningly.

"Sandy's crying because she's so happy," I told him, shrugging my shoulders.

"That happens sometimes. It's one way of showing emotion." He didn't sound at all surprised and I was grateful to him for handling the situation.

By then, several other kids had started to gather around us, but Peter waved them off. He gently put one hand on Sandy's shoulder and with his other, he handed her his handkerchief.

"Thanks," she mumbled, wiping her eyes and blowing her nose. The next thing I knew, Sandy was actually smiling, and she apologized for carrying on.

"I'm used to emotional women," Peter assured her. "My kid sister is twelve and she's either laughing or crying."

"But I'm not twelve." Sandy was indignant.

"No, but we've all been under a strain."

"I promise I'll get your hanky back to you, washed and pressed."

"Don't worry, Sandy. I have a huge supply. Standard equipment for pianists."

"Hey, we better get going or they might run out of food," Sandy advised, now completely recovered.

She hurried away, and Peter and I were left alone. I was truly astonished at how he'd taken over so masterfully and without thinking, I said, "You were wonderful."

He smiled shyly, the "old" Peter, and without a word put his hand on my arm and guided me through the door to the east hall. The reception room was jammed with wall-to-wall maroon-jacketed boys, sprinkled with members of our group. There was a long table filled with tea sandwiches, crumpets, biscuits, scones and other English delectables, including huge urns of coffee and tea. We instinctively headed for it, but somehow we got separated.

There was quite a crunch at the table and after I helped myself to a scone and a cup of tea, I gingerly moved away toward a relatively uncrowded space. I immediately was surrounded by half-a-dozen St. George boys who congratulated me on my performance. "Good show!" the tallest and probably oldest, a blond stringbean, remarked. "Jolly good," the smaller ones echoed.

"You were a wonderful audience," I told them. That must have been the right thing to say, because they were all smiles and the ice had been broken. After that, they barraged me with questions.

"How long do you have to rehearse?" "Where are you singing next?" "Is Bryant High School very different from St. George's?" "What's it like at a coed school?"

I was so absorbed in answering their questions that I was reluctant to leave when the word was passed that it was time to go. Julie tapped me on the shoulder and pointed toward the door.

"One more minute," I begged.

"Just one," she mouthed, and moved away.

Sabrina was passing by and must have witnessed the whole scene because she spoke to Julie in a voice loud enough for me to hear, "I hope there aren't special rules for the so-called stars."

I was determined to ignore her and finished answering one little boy's query about whether he could write me a letter at Bryant High School.

"I'd love to hear from you," I told him, "and I promise I'll write back."

Then I said goodbye, rushed off, collected my things, and boarded the bus.

"Sit down wherever you can," Clyde ordered, "so that I can count noses."

I slid into a seat next to Greta, and couldn't help thinking of Sabrina's remark. I must have looked glum, because Greta, who I hadn't spoken to since the concert, asked, "Why aren't you smiling? I thought you were terrific and you didn't even look scared."

"I was terrified, until I began singing," I confessed.

"Then you should be really pleased with yourself."

"Not everyone would agree with you."

Greta looked at me oddly but she didn't know what to say. I think we were both relieved when the bus took off and the kids broke into a medley of Beatles songs. I joined in and by the time we arrived at Westminster Bridge I was once again caught up in the good feelings generated by our first success. Then, when I got off the bus, Mr. Saxe pulled me aside and said, "You've got the makings of a real pro, Beth. Keep it up."

"I'll try as hard as I can," I promised. And as soon as I said that I realized that it didn't matter what Sabrina thought about me. The important thing was that I sang well, and the closer I could come to being a "star" the better.

There was a mist over the Thames, a typical London night. It was the perfect background for the final scene in those old English movies where the hero, usually a foreign correspondent wearing a trench coat and a slouch hat, must leave his beloved and go off to the front. It was impossible not to think romantic thoughts in such an atmosphere, and quite naturally I drew parallels between the leading players in the movie, and Tom and me. Tom was called to duty by his job, and I was his forsaken lover. I was trying to figure out a happier ending for my scenario, when Patsy called.

"Get in line, Beth. We have to cue up, you know."

"Oh, sure," I muttered, and drifted to the end of the line.

I hadn't been listening, but apparently Tom had purchased all the tickets and was passing them out as we crossed the gangplank of the small cruiser. It occurred to me that he hadn't spoken to me since the concert, but then my "hero" was busy attending to other matters. Although I hadn't really planned it that way, since I was the last in line, except for Clyde who remained in back looking for strays, Tom and I boarded together.

There were seats above and below deck, and Tom headed directly for the top deck of the stern. Of course, I followed. In spite of the mist, it was still light and we had an impressionistic view of the city that gave it a fairyland quality. It was probably just as well I wasn't alone with Tom because in my weakened condition, based upon the excitement of the last twenty-four hours, and my feelings for Tom, I might have dissolved.

The rows were already half filled with members of the choir, and any hopes I had of having a private conversation with Tom rapidly faded. Kiki was seated behind us, and as soon as the boat was released from its moorings, she asked Tom, "Where are we? Where are we going? What's that building over there?"

"Hang in, Kiki, and I'll give you my ten-pound lecture on the Thames for free," Tom said.

"I can tell you about the fish," Evan volunteered in his dry, scientific manner. And without waiting for any encouragement, he informed us that the increase in sewage from the increasing population and the effluent from the factories since the turn of the century had killed off the fish life with the exception of "an occasional eel."

"Yuck!" Sandy commented.

"However," Evan continued, "new anti-pollution laws of the sixties have changed all that. Now smelt, shrimps, salmon, and seahorses abound."

"Wouldn't think so to look at this murky water," Mike stated. He and Flos were sitting in front of us, holding hands, and I envied how at ease they were together.

"Some say the murk is due to silt, not pollution," Evan explained. "Anything else I can tell you?"

Tom ended an embarrassing pause. "Evan has given you an expert account of what's going on underwater. Now I'll try to tell you what's happening on the surface. We're just passing the Victoria Embankment, and across the river is County Hall, the Shell Building, and Festival Hall. The latter boasts some of the finest musical events in London, ballet, orchestral, you name it."

He went on about Old Watergate of York House, and Cleopatra's Needle, which has nothing to do with Cleopatra, St. Paul's Cathedral—London's largest and most famous church—the Houses of Parliament, and "Big Ben," the 320-foot clock tower that is the universal symbol of London.

Tom seemed to know absolutely everything about London, and as far as I was concerned, he could have gone on forever with a detailed description of every crypt, crown, and cloister. I hung on to every word and therefore, when he glanced at his watch and abruptly stopped talking, I hoped he didn't notice my disappointment.

"I'm going on too long," he apologized.

"No, you're not," Kiki cried.

"Not at all," Priscilla chimed in. Obviously, I wasn't the only one who was riveted.

"But I have to see how the rest of the troops are faring." He moved off, and there was no way he could have been persuaded to stay. I pretended not to care, and as he headed for the bow, I made a special point of going in the opposite direction. I knew I was being ridiculous, but I was sure he had planned a rendezvous with Sabrina. So what, my more reasonable self argued. But as I leaned against the gunwale and gazed across the Thames, my eyes filled with tears. It was so overwhelming: how could everything be so wonderful and so terrible at the same time? I was so filled with emotion that I didn't notice anyone approach until I felt a hand on my shoulder. It was Peter, who looked at me with such understanding that I knew he was aware I was in some sort of turmoil.

"You were beautiful tonight," he breathed.

"You mean my singing?"

"I mean . . . I mean . . ."

Then, as though he couldn't bring himself to say anything else, he turned away, leaving me more baffled than ever.

Seven hours of uninterrupted sleep restored my equilibrium, and when I woke up the next morning, my problems no longer seemed insurmountable. Daisy was still sound asleep, so I washed and dressed as quietly as possible and went downstairs to breakfast. Not surprisingly, I found myself alone in the dining room, which had just opened.

After I helped myself to the self-service breakfast, I

sat down at a window table, took the day's schedule out of my bag, and studied it. We were programmed for a free morning, then back to the hotel for a rehearsal in the afternoon, and an informal concert at an old age home that evening. I was munching on a biscuit and idly staring out the window when Tom, rather noisily, sat down opposite me. He radared his smile at me, and I had trouble not choking on my biscuit even though I had drowned it in honey.

"You're a lark, like me," he began.

"A lark?"

"At Cambridge, we were categorized as either larks or owls. Loosely translated, that means morning or night people."

"And I'm a lark?"

"In more ways than one. Not only are you an early bird, but you sing like a dream."

"Thank you, Tom. I didn't know you heard me."

The minute that slipped out, I regretted it. I was sure a flicker of annoyance crossed his face, and I didn't blame him. There was no reason for me to expect Tom to go out of his way to compliment me. I was just one of twenty-four students and there were all those courier rules. Besides, after this tour, he'd be on to something else. I'd never see him again.

As though he were reading my mind and wanted to dispel my misgivings, he leaned over and said in a low voice, "I hope that the end of this trip doesn't mean I'll never see you again, Beth." He sounded so sincere I thought I must have imagined his being annoyed with me seconds before.

"I wish I could believe that," I told him. "There's no way I'll be coming back to England for years."

"But maybe I'll find a way to get to the States."

"You mean it?" I exclaimed. "How?"

"I'm trying to figure out a way I could get there next summer."

"I could get behind that," I said, as evenly as possible. The mere suggestion that Tom would be on my turf, that I'd see him again, made me shiver with excitement. I wanted to know more about his plans, but a number of kids had come down to breakfast and Tom straightened back in his chair, making it obvious that our private conversation was finished.

"Better reinforce myself with some tea," he said, grinning. "Can I get you anything?"

"No thanks," I answered. I couldn't swallow another morsel. I just wanted to sit back and revel in the idea that possibly I would see him again after the tour. The way he had phrased it—*I hope that the end of this trip doesn't mean I'll never see you again, Beth*—implied that it was *me* he wanted to see in the States.

I watched him thread his way toward the breakfast spread. I was feeling so confident about him that it didn't even bother me when Sabrina, whose table he was passing on his way, possessively reached for his arm, pulled him toward her, and whispered something in his ear. By the time he'd refilled his teacup, at least half-a-dozen girls—I observed that boys rarely needed him—had found some excuse to talk to him. It didn't look like he'd ever get back to my table, so I figured there was no point for me to hang around. I swiped an orange and biscuit for Daisy and went back to our room. She had one eye open and gratefully accepted my food offering.

"Ridiculous to get up so early," she complained. "Especially when we have a free morning."

"But there's so much to see! We've got to get started."

"Right on," Patsy yelled from the door. "As soon as

I tank up on tea, I shall return. Daisy will be pulled together, and we can map out our exploration strategy."

"Good thinking," I shouted after her fleeting figure. Then I turned to Daisy. "Up, up, up," I commanded.

"Oh, you two," Daisy groaned. "Where would I be if it weren't for you?"

"Asleep, and hungry."

"You win," she chuckled, and flew into action.

As soon as Patsy returned, we made our plan. The "musts" were the British Museum, Buckingham Palace, hopefully in time for the changing of the guards, Madame Tussaud's Waxworks, and Harrods' Department Store.

"That's the proper blend of culture and couture," Patsy surmised.

"But I've got to visit Poets' Corner in Westminster Abbey. My father will never forgive me if I don't. Tennyson, Milton, and Shakespeare are memorialized there," Daisy told us.

"And I want to visit the Tate Gallery. My mother says it has masterpieces of everything from William Blake and Turner to Degas and Warhol," I said.

"Well personally, I'd like to visit the zoo," Patsy stated. "But we can't do everything."

"I've got a neat idea," I offered. "Why don't we do as much as we can together until noon, and then split up. We don't have to be back here until two for rehearsal, and we can survive the wilds of London alone for a couple of hours."

"Genius idea," Patsy roared.

And Daisy added, "Sheer brilliance."

"Of course, I'm not sure how you two will make out in this foreign country without me as a translator," Patsy said, deadpanned.

"What do you mean, without you . . ." I began. Then I realized I'd fallen into her trap and we had one of our usual giggling fits which lasted until we got downstairs and asked the concierge the best way to go to our various destinations. The concierge, who looked like a scaled-down version of Robert Morley, but who had the traces of a Cockney accent, patiently explained what buses we should take, and we were off.

There was no use pretending we could even begin to "cover" the British Museum, but Patsy, who had brought a guidebook and was fast becoming our peerless leader, quoted from it: "See what you can, and savor what you see in the hope that you can return again."

"We'll begin with the Elgin Marbles," Patsy directed, her head buried in the guidebook. "It says here these original carvings, part of the Parthenon, were brought from Greece in the nineteenth century by the Earl of Elgin. Then we'll visit the Egyptian Collection, which displays the Rosetta Stone, a work that has helped archeologists interpret Egyptian script. There are a zillion other collections, including Assyrian, Greek, Roman, British, Medieval, Oriental antiquities, to say nothing of the British Library, which has several million books—rare illuminated volumes among them— and makes this one of the greatest libraries in the world."

"You're beginning to bore us," Daisy dared to say. "Isn't she, Beth?"

"Yes," I nodded.

"It's too bad my best friends have to be cultural cretins," Patsy sighed. But then she smiled, and said decisively, "Since you won't listen, I might just as well show you these treasures. That way, something might sink in. Follow me!"

Patsy showed us the highlights of the museum. Then we went to Buckingham Palace and caught the tail end of the changing of the guard, which exceeded our picture-book expectations. Next, we were awed by Madame Tussaud's Waxworks, especially the resemblances of the American presidents. It was almost noon when we shared a taxi to Harrods', where Patsy, who by now we had nicknamed Nanny because she had been so strict, let us loose.

I just wanted to roam around and drink in the most elegant department store I'd ever seen. Patsy told us Harrods' food emporium was known for its exotic delicacies, and she might bring her parents some venison or quail or candied grasshoppers. And Daisy had to check out the dried flowers. "Imagine if I could find an arrangement of daisies and roses for my mother," she exclaimed.

"We just have to go our separate ways," Patsy allowed. "I hope you can fend for yourselves."

"It won't be easy," I said, half seriously.

"We couldn't have gotten this far without you, Nanny," Daisy remarked.

"If it hadn't been for me, you'd probably still be hanging around the sarcophaguses in the British Museum, unable to find your way out!"

"You're right, Nanny," Daisy and I said in unison, and then the three of us did our best to control our borderline hysteria. The last thing we wanted to do was make a "scene" in snobby Harrods', and in order to avoid that possibility, we mumbled something about seeing each other later and quickly went off in opposite directions.

As I ambled along the luxuriously appointed floors, my mind boggled at the glittering array of merchandise. There were an endless number of departments, all so plush that they were a little intimidating. I almost couldn't imagine buying anything in such a rarified atmosphere. However, I could understand why Harrods', reputedly, was the Queen's favorite place to do her Christmas shopping.

It was about one o'clock when I finished "casing" Harrods' and no time for the Tate, which I mentally promised myself I would visit another day. When I got outside, I was dazzled by the sparkling clear day, and although I'd loved being with my two best friends it was delicious to be on my own. I could wend my way back to our hotel at my own tortoiselike pace, soak in the English ambience, and melt into the crowd. I knew the hotel was less than a half-hour away, which meant I had time to make a slight detour to Hyde Park, and stroll along the Serpentine, a lake shaped like a croissant, in the middle of the bustling city. It seemed like an oasis for everyone: mothers and children, office workers, couples.

I sat down on a bench by the lake and watched some kids floating a miniature sailboat. I'd been so high all morning that I hadn't had much time to think about Tom, but now I missed him. Also, I suddenly felt limp with fatigue; the blister on my heel which I had tried to ignore was killing me; I hadn't had anything to eat since early morning; and I was beginning to feel the heat. Much as I relished pretending I was an English schoolgirl, I knew I had better get some nourishment and make tracks back to the hotel, or risk being totally wrecked during the rehearsal.

On the way out of the park, a vendor was selling ices, and I bought an ice cream sandwich. It started to dissolve before I'd gone even a block, so I ducked under the awning of a tiny souvenir shop in order to prevent my "lunch" from disappearing completely. As

I worked on the sandwich, I looked over the zillion trinkets on view in the window and idly wondered who bought such bric-a-brac. What a foolish way to spend money, I thought, when my eye caught a key chain with a Cupid attached. It looked exactly like the statue at Piccadilly Circus, and might have been the Angel of Christian Charity that Tom had described our first night on the town.

I had to buy it for Tom! It was a silly gift, but that was exactly why I could give it to him. He could accept it any way he wanted—as a trivial thought or a meaningful remembrance. I felt energized again, quickly finished my ice cream, popped into the store, and for fifty pence, that absurd-looking plastic angel was mine.

I hurried back to the hotel in the naive hope that I would find Tom there alone, but there was no sign of him in the lobby, the restaurant, or the rehearsal room. I still had twenty minutes until rehearsal time, and this was a perfect opportunity for me to take advantage of our community bathroom, which was rarely unoccupied. I grabbed my towel and some clean clothes, and raced down the hall. After I luxuriated in the shower and shampooed my hair, I put on my fresh clothes, wrapped my dripping hair in the towel, and felt ready to face anything . . . anything, that was, except Tom, who was leaping down the stairs two at a time, and muttering under his breath. He stopped cold when he saw me going back to my room and I could feel myself blush. This was not the romantic meeting I had envisioned: strands of hair that must have looked like wet spaghetti sticking out of my towel, my shirt sticking out of my jeans, and barefoot.

"You should always wear turbans," he observed, chuckling. "You have the perfect cheekbones."

"I do," I said, not sure whether he was making fun of me or not.

"Absolutely! Anyhow, I don't want to hold you up and I have to report to the management about the lift. The flaming thing has conked out. The capacity is four, but it doesn't say four what—probably pygmies!"

That made me laugh and I wasn't quite so self-conscious. Also, I thought kismet had played a role in our meeting alone like this, and I'd better take advantage of it.

I scrounged in my pocket for the angel and handed it to him, trying to hide my embarrassment. "Just like the one in Piccadilly," I reminded him.

He looked at it bemusedly, and then remarked, "It's charming . . . just the way you look right now."

I wanted to take him seriously, but I knew he was teasing, or was he? We could hear hordes of kids climbing up the stairs, and Tom swiftly stuffed the key chain in his pocket, planted a quick kiss on my cheek, and whispered, "Later."

I stood there, mesmerized, until he disappeared down the stairs. Then, still in a daze, I drifted into my room and sank down on the bed. I might have stayed there forever if Daisy hadn't burst into the room, urging me to put on my shoes and untangle my hair.

"We've only got two minutes," she cried. "I think this British air has affected your metabolism."

"You're so right," I said agreeably. "I don't think I'll ever be the same."

6

It seemed everytime I had a sense of proportion about Tom, he'd do something that totally threw me. That kiss, for example. You could hardly call it that—a firm handshake would have been equally romantic—but I couldn't get it out of my mind. And maybe next time it would be a real kiss, with his lips pressed against mine, and his arms around me. Just thinking about that possibility made me weak all over, but first things first. I had to get to rehearsal!

I frantically pulled a comb through my hair and slipped into some sandals. Fortunately, because of the broken lift, Mr. Saxe gave us five minutes grace, and I wasn't the last one to get in place. I was operating on nervous energy and felt slightly intoxicated. Actually, I think my brain had been affected by my feelings for Tom, because I did something in rehearsal that I never did before in my life. Because of Tom, the words of love seemed especially poignant, and in my infatuated state of mind I recklessly changed the sex in a madrigal by Thomas Morley. The original line, "My bonnie lass she smileth/ When she my heart beguileth," I sang as, "My bonnie lad he smileth/ When he my heart beguileth."

I didn't think anyone noticed, but during the break Helene, who was standing next to me in the soprano section, made a crack about some people not knowing the difference between a lad and a lass. I felt like such an airhead that I couldn't say anything in my defense, but I vowed never to mess around with the text again.

When the rehearsal was over, Tom announced that we should be ready to board the bus at five, the concert would take place as soon as we arrived in Hampstead, "the Golden Oldies can't wait" is the way he put it, then a half hour of chatting up the residents, and a bus ride back to the hotel. "You're on your own for dinner, and if you decide to hang around Hampstead, please let Clyde know."

As soon as he was finished speaking, Patsy and Peter came running over to me. "We want to get a group together to go to a Chinese restaurant after the concert," Patsy began.

"It's right near the old age home, and according to Patsy's guidebook, it has terrific Cantonese food. Interested?" Peter asked.

"Sure," I replied.

"Come on, Peter, we have to scrape up some other Chinese food freaks," Patsy ordered, pulling him away. "I know we can count on Daisy."

"We need some more guys," Peter said. "I can't handle three women all by myself."

I was dying to say, "Why don't you invite Tom?" but that would have been too bold. Besides, Tom undoubtedly had other obligations. I wanted to put him out of my mind during the bus ride, but that was impossible because as soon as we sat down Kiki pleaded with him to tell us about Hampstead. Then, for most of the ride, Tom described, in his devastatingly charming manner, the features of Hampstead. "It tops a hill and is famous for its vast heath that you colonists would call a humungus park," and my heart was more beguiled than ever.

The old people in the home, all at least in their eighties, had skin like papier-mâché, missing teeth, and half of them were in wheelchairs, but they had an extraordinary twinkle in their eyes when we sang, and couldn't get enough of us. Mr. Saxe had purposely planned a short program, but they begged for encores, and he happily obliged.

When it came time for the "chatting up," I noticed a hunched-over old man with a cane dodder over to Peter, who was still seated at the piano. Peter made room for him on the bench, and I heard the man say in a croaking voice, "I used to play in a music hall. 'It's a Long Way to Tipperary' was one of my specialties."

"I happen to know that!" Peter exclaimed, and began playing that well-known English tune.

The elderly man sang along in a monotone, and he looked so happy that I could feel a lump in my throat. "Thank you, thank you," he muttered, when the piece was finished. "I didn't think I'd ever get a chance to sing that again." Then he got up and hobbled over to an easy chair at the side of the room, settled into it, pulled out a tattered gray handkerchief, and wiped a tear from his eye.

I was so absorbed by this sight that I was startled when I felt a tap on my shoulder.

"Didn't mean to frighten you." It was Tom.

"Oh, hi," I said, trying to orient myself to his presence.

"You look like you're getting into this."

"I am. I've never been in a home like this and I'm amazed at how appreciative everyone is."

"It's not my cup of tea," he grumbled.

As we were talking, an ancient white-haired woman wearing a hearing aid and using a walker, said as she inched past us, "Such beautiful music. I never heard such beautiful music. Like angels . . ."

"See what I mean by grateful?" I whispered to Tom.

"I personally like my women a bit younger, specifically about six inches shorter than me, with dark hair and gray eyes."

"Whoever could that be?" I surprised myself at how coy I was.

"We could discuss this in depth on the bus on the way back to the hotel."

"Isn't that against the rules for couriers?"

"I've been known to cheat a little. And if you come to supper later with some kids I've promised to take to a Fish 'n' Chips place, I'll make up for my peccadillo."

"How?"

"I'll pay very little attention to you, but you'll know how I'm feeling."

"Well, er, I had promised Patsy and . . ."

"If you care about me, you'll get out of whatever you promised."

I care about you terribly, I thought, and I'm willing to lie, rob, cheat—do whatever you want—to please you. Aloud, I said, "I'll try and get out of it."

"Good show. Be one of the last ones to board the bus, take a seat in the rear, and we'll have a little time together."

I was intrigued, thrilled and guilt-ridden all at the same time, but I couldn't resist joining in the complicity. I would manufacture an excuse that would prevent me from hurting anyone's feelings, at least that was my justification for signaling to Patsy, who was talking to an old lady in a wheelchair.

"What's wrong?" she asked, after indicating to the old woman that she was being summoned by me.

"I don't feel too great," I said, "and I don't think I can handle Chinese food. I think I'll go back to the hotel." I couldn't look her in the eye and made a big deal of reading my watch as though I just learned how to tell time.

"That's too bad, but I'm sure we can find something less exotic than Cantonese. Maybe there's an Italian restaurant around. I'll go get Peter, who's still hanging onto my guidebook."

"That's okay. I mean I'm not in the mood to eat anything."

"What did you have for lunch?"

"An ice cream sandwich."

"No wonder you feel funny. You're probably starving. You'll fade away from malnutrition if you keep this up. I promise you we'll find a place that will offer just the right thing to improve your gastrointestinal indisposition."

"No, really, Patsy. I think I better go back and take it easy." I was getting more and more uncomfortable, and also slightly annoyed with her insistence, even though I knew she meant well.

"But you have to eat," she persisted.

"I don't have to do anything. And stop being so bossy," I snapped.

Patsy looked at me quizzically, slowly accepting the

fact that I wasn't kidding. "Okay," she said softly, "I guess you know what's best for you."

"I better get going now. All the 'bus' people will be boarding soon." I felt awful that I'd lied and it was hard to keep my voice from quivering.

Patsy turned around abruptly and stalked off without another word. I knew she was angry and I was tempted to run after her, but the idea that Tom was expecting me was more important than anything. I'd square things with Patsy later, apologize for barking at her, and make a point of languishing in bed by the time she returned to the hotel.

I remembered Tom's instructions, to be one of the last to pile into the bus, and to take a seat in the back. I waited . . . and waited . . . and waited. I was getting more and more jittery and finally I stood up in the aisle, wanting to make sure he saw me, and also to find out where he was sitting. If he was with another girl— especially Sabrina—I would be ready to kill. Fortunately, for him, for her, and for my blood pressure, he was sitting next to Mr. Saxe and I knew there was no way he could get back to me.

I brooded about my bad luck all the way to London, and vaguely wondered if I was being punished. However, when we arrived, Tom made a special point of waiting for me and I thought the trip, which had been a bummer in every sense, was worth it.

"Sorry, love," he said, "but I had to ask Mr. Saxe something about the scheduling for the next couple of days. I had no idea it would take so long."

"You mean you started the discussion when you knew I was waiting for you?" It was hard not to show my irritation.

"But Beth, I was a captive audience and couldn't get

away. You know that I wanted to be with you more than anything." He gently squeezed my arm and I felt tingly all over.

"It was so lonesome back there," I said, working on his sympathy.

"I'll make it up to you, Beth."

"Promise?"

"With all my heart," he murmured.

I thought he was really going to kiss me then, because everyone had wandered into the hotel, and he bent his head toward me. But a split second before our lips touched, a loud voice called from the lobby. "Hey, Tom, the troops are champing at the bit. We're all waiting for you." It was Clyde, acting in the line of duty, but destroying my romance in the process. Was everyone, inadvertently, conspiring to keep Tom and me apart?

"I'm coming," Tom shouted. He looked at me longingly, then briskly turned and went into the hotel while I stood outside like a deserted sick puppy.

When the group, about seven kids, sauntered out, I fell in with them as inconspicuously as possible. I was hungry, I didn't want to be alone, and at least I'd be at the same table with Tom even if he paid no attention to me. The restaurant was about six blocks away, on an obscure street, but was obviously well known because we had to wait fifteen minutes for a table. The sawdust on the floor and plastic flowers on the oilcloth table-cloths created a less than elegant feeling but the fish 'n' chips, fried fillet of fish and French fried potato chips, were superb.

I was in a subdued mood and didn't feel much like contributing to the conversation. Fortunately, Evan was seated next to me and was going on about the effects of heredity on longevity. As we ambled home, he explained to me a formula for figuring out how long one will live based on one's grandparents' age, eating and exercise habits, and education. To my surprise, I got caught up in what he was saying and wasn't aware of how much walking we'd done until the hotel loomed in front of me. Then, to my horror, I saw Patsy, Peter and Daisy, with a few others, approaching the hotel entrance from the opposite direction. I had read in novels about people in embarrassing situations wanting the ground to open and swallow them up, but I didn't think that ever occurred in real life. However, that was exactly what I wished would happen to me. I wanted to disappear!

I realized that the distance to the restaurant, the wait for the table, and the slow service accounted for me not getting back to the hotel ahead of Patsy and company. They had taken the tube from Hampstead, which was much shorter than the bus ride, but still I never thought I wouldn't return before them.

The only thing I could do was hang back, but of course they saw me and made a point of waiting for me to catch up to them. Patsy stared at me as though she had seen a ghost. "That's the fastest recuperation on record," she remarked, and brushed by me into the hotel.

"I thought you were sick," Daisy said, frowning. "In fact, that's one of the reasons we hurried back."

"That's right," Peter confirmed. "We even brought you 100 ingredients soup wrapped in foil to keep it warm. We figured that one of those ingredients might cure you." He looked baffled and concerned, and that made me feel guiltier than ever. What had started out as a little white lie had turned into a major deception of nightmare quality.

"I don't understand you, Beth. I just don't understand you," Daisy said, and she disappeared into the hotel.

"You must have had your reasons," Peter observed, sympathetically. Those were the only comforting words anyone had spoken, and I wanted to rush into his arms and place my head on his shoulder. But I had enough presence of mind to know that would embarrass him. Also, I was on the verge of weeping and didn't want anyone to see me. I ran into the hotel, raced up the stairs into my room, and gave into an impulse I hadn't had since I was six years old: I threw myself on the bed, buried my head under the pillow, and sobbed, and sobbed, and sobbed.

I don't know how long I stayed that way, but when Daisy came into the room I was still lying on the bed fully clothed. The room was dark but she knew I was there. She asked in a low voice, "Are you sleeping?"

"No," I answered. "Just thinking. I hope you're still talking to me."

"Well, I am, but I think you should know that Patsy's really ticked off. I've spent the last half hour trying to defend you. Problem is, I don't have too many terrific arguments for your case."

She had turned on the light, and I slowly swung my legs over the side of the bed and came to a sitting position. I felt punch-drunk—my eyes were swollen from crying and my nose was red.

"You look awful," Daisy observed.

"Thanks," I said, and almost smiled.

"Go wash your face. You'll feel better. And I've still got this 100 ingredients soup, slightly on the cool side now, but it'll be a new taste sensation."

"You are my best friend," I sighed, and almost broke into tears again.

Then I went to the sink, covered my face with soap, splashed cold water on it at least twenty times, and blotted it dry. After that, I brushed my hair vigorously, changed into my nightshirt, and felt almost human.

"You want to try this?" Daisy asked, offering me a soggy carton of soup.

"You, first," I said.

"We got it for you, remember?"

I didn't have the strength to argue, so I took a small sip and tried not to make a face.

"Your turn," I said.

Daisy took a swallow, and then plunged toward the sink to spit it out. "Yuck," she choked out, "that's the most awful tasting stuff."

Since I never thought I'd smile again, I was amazed to find myself chuckling while Daisy poured the remains down the sink. "Are you okay?" I asked.

"I'll live, I guess. In spite of all appearances, I wasn't trying to poison you."

"Wouldn't blame you if you did," I conceded.

"You still haven't explained why you stood us up, although I've got a pretty good idea."

"You probably know, since I've always thought you were a mindreader."

"I don't think I'd have to have any extraordinary perceptions to know it had something to do with Tom."

"You guessed it."

"But why lie?"

"Because I didn't want to hurt anybody's feelings. I mean I couldn't come out and say to Patsy I had a more interesting offer."

"Yes, you could, but you didn't. I mean if Greg suddenly appeared on the scene, I'd sacrifice family, friends, fame, and fortune just to spend an hour with him."

"One other thing, though. I know you don't quite approve of Tom for me."

"That's not what we're talking about," she said, skillfully avoiding the issue of Tom. "Anyhow, it's getting late and we have to leave at the crack of dawn for Salsgate. It's a three-hour bus ride."

"I know," I said, climbing into bed.

I watched Daisy disappear into the hall on her way to the bathroom and thought how much better I felt having talked to her. She seemed to understand my behavior, even if she didn't approve. And I sensed that Peter would forgive me even without an explanation. But I wasn't so sure about Patsy, who saw everything in black and white. Tom, who had gotten me into this mess, didn't even know about it, and as I was falling off to sleep, I decided I'd never tell him. If I got so upset over something that he would probably consider insignificant, he might be totally turned off.

I fell into a dreamless sleep, and then woke the next morning before Daisy, in spite of having been wrung out by the previous night's drama. I quietly got dressed, slipped out of the room, and went downstairs to breakfast.

Because we had to pack and be off for Salsgate by nine o'clock, there were already several members of the choir in the dining room. I exchanged greetings with a few kids, filled my tray with a Continental breakfast of rolls and tea, and automatically headed for "our" table near the window. I was concentrating so hard on not spilling my tea that I was halfway there before I looked up and saw it was occupied—by *them*—Tom and Sabrina. They were so involved going halfies on their croissant and muffin, that they didn't notice me. I could feel my hands begin to shake and frantically looked around for a place to put my tray before I dropped it.

There were still a lot of empty tables and since I wanted to get as far away from them as possible, I hurried to a far corner of the room. I didn't want Tom to see me sitting alone, if he ever bothered to take his eyes off Sabrina, and when I saw Peter at a table for two against the wall, I zeroed in on him.

"Do you mind if I sit here?" I gasped, hoping he didn't notice how flustered I was.

"Course not," he replied warmly, and made room for my tray.

I was relieved that he didn't seem to bear a grudge against me, but I still felt I had to make some explanation about how I'd behaved.

"About last night . . ." I began.

"You don't have to explain, Beth, or maybe I don't want to know."

His eyes clouded for an instant, but then he quickly got off the subject. "Did you try the 100 ingredients soup?"

"Daisy and I decided that it takes a cultivated palate, but I really appreciate your thinking of me."

He didn't know what to say and busily buttered his English muffin, his head bent, averting my eyes. Then, taking a deep breath, he raised his head and stared at me so hard I thought he was about to make some momentous pronouncement. Therefore, I was surprised, and a little amused, when he said, "These English muffins are delicious. Very different from those in the States. Would you take half of mine?"

"Only if you'll take half of my sweet roll."

"Deal," he agreed, putting half his muffin on my plate.

"Bartering food seems to be an American custom." It was Tom's unmistakable voice behind me and I tried not to overreact. Apparently, he'd been watching this whole transaction.

"You ought to know," I remarked, sounding much more shrill than I intended. No matter how hard I tried, I couldn't be natural with Tom.

"I was the first one in the dining room," he pointed out, a remark which must have seemed like a non sequitur to Peter, but which had great significance for me. It meant that he had expected me to be waiting for him at our table. It wasn't his fault if Sabrina got there ahead of me and took over.

"Tom, do I have time to wash my hair?" It was Flos, who had wandered over, looking spacier than ever.

Before he could answer, Kiki came running up, shouting that the zipper on her suitcase was broken and she needed a rope to hold it together.

Then Helene stuck her head in the door of the dining room and screamed, "Tom, I sent my only dress to be dry-cleaned and it's not back yet."

Tom sighed wearily and moved away from our table. "One at a time," he pleaded, "one at a time."

Peter and I looked at each other and cracked up. It was a relief to stop sparring with Tom, and to find myself laughing with Peter. I was beginning to see him not only as a terrific musician, and someone I could count on, but as a very special friend.

After being fortified with breakfast, Peter's unquestioning acceptance of my childish deception, and Tom's oblique explanation of why he was sitting with Sabrina, life was no longer unbearable. In fact, I felt almost cheerful as I dumped my tray and dishes in the "used" receptacle and then picked out a roll and banana to bring to Daisy.

I was actually humming as I trudged up the stairs,

thinking that I must have exaggerated the "sin" I had committed. By the time I reached our floor I had practically convinced myself that I hadn't done anything so terrible, until I saw Patsy. She was heading for the staircase and I waited until she was less than two feet away from me before greeting her. But she didn't respond, she didn't even look at me; she just grazed past me as though I were a non-person.

I felt like a deflated balloon when I shuffled into our room. Daisy was half-dressed and brushing her teeth. "Hiya," she sputtered cheerfully, glancing at the roll and banana which I placed on the dresser, "I appreciate the room service."

"That's okay," I mumbled despondently. Then I dragged my suitcase onto the bed and started stuffing it with my belongings.

"You don't look too happy," she said, sitting on her bed and peeling the banana. "Were there repercussions this morning?"

"Peter was a sweetie, and I thought the whole incident would be forgotten until I saw Patsy in the hall just now. Talk about 'frost in May'! She's not speaking to me, so how can I explain?"

"You know Patsy. She'll come around eventually."

"I hope so."

"You can't let it ruin your trip. Besides, you're the one who kept telling me the important thing about this tour is the performance, and singing, and dedication, and the virtue of hard work, and on and on and on." She was mocking me and had trouble keeping a straight face, and I couldn't help laughing at myself. The truth was, I had said all those things at one time or another, and I really believed them. But that was before Tom. If love was supposed to make the world go round, why was I finding it so shattering? It had already forced me to be devious, to threaten my close friendships, to make me suspicious. If this was what love accomplished, who needed it? I asked myself. But I knew that was a foolish question. I was hooked on Tom, and no amount of reasoning or common sense could change my feelings.

7

I wasn't feeling very sociable so I took a seat next to Priscilla, whom I could trust not to chatter the entire trip. We dozed off almost immediately, but once we were out of London, I felt a gentle tap on my shoulder and slowly opened my eyes. It was Peter, who was sitting behind us. He had also awakened Pris, and then he reminded us that we might never be in this part of the world again.

"You're right," I acknowledged, "but I can't seem to keep my eyes open."

"Me, either," Pris sighed.

"I have just the thing," he said, and offered us a chocolate bar.

Pris and I shared it, and agreed that it tasted better than any we'd had in the States.

"I think you're the most thoughtful person on this trip," Pris told him in her straightforward manner.

I didn't have to turn around to know that Peter would be dying of embarrassment. "Easy," he remarked. "All I did was provide you with instant energy."

"Just what we needed. We'd be missing all this absolutely lovely country—cows, sheep, villages. It looks like it's sprung full-blown out of a picture book," I added.

By now, Pris and I were fully awake, and considering how antisocial I'd been feeling, it was surprising how much we chatted the rest of the trip. I was still upset about Patsy, but that was the last thing I wanted to talk about. However, when we stopped at an inn just before Salsgate for a plowman's lunch of cheese, lettuce, and bread, I hoped she'd make some sign of friendship. But she was decidedly cool and I knew I had no choice but to take Daisy's advice and wait until she came around, if she ever did.

My worries about Patsy temporarily diminished when the bus pulled up to Salsgate, an honest-to-goodness medieval castle where we would be staying for the next few days. It wouldn't have surprised me if King Arthur and Guinevere were in residence, it so closely resembled what I dreamed to be Camelot.

The castle was used as a school in the winter, but the stables had been converted into bedrooms to accommodate tours, according to the gnomelike man and his wife who greeted us. The couple introduced themselves as castle managers and took enormous pride in every inch of their responsibility, from the elaborate suits of armor that lined the entrance hall, to the turret that topped the roof.

After the confinement of the bus, we all went a little ape when we learned we would be assigned stalls.

Timmy, a short bass who had kept a very low profile until that moment, suddenly began neighing and pawing at the ground. A number of others were inspired by his example, and soon half the choir was acting out "horsey," while the rest of us were convulsed with laughter. The castle managers looked rather alarmed, and Tom, with what I considered unusual aplomb, authoritatively asked us to stop "horsing" around so that he could tell us our program.

"There will be a short rehearsal from four to five in the Gold Room, supper in the dining hall at six, and at seven-thirty we will walk to a nearby eleventh century church for concert."

"You could get lost in this place," Kiki observed, looking around the enormous hall where we were standing. "And there are so many doorways."

"Not to worry," Tom assured her. "Mr. Gorley here, our castle manager, has kindly consented to conduct us through his palace."

I thought it was particularly clever of Tom to refer to Salsgate as Mr. Gorley's palace, although he obviously didn't own it. Mr. Gorley beamed with pride, and formally nodding his head in our direction said, "I will be only too happy to escort you through these majestic halls."

"Clyde, keeper of the keys, will assign you your rooms. Be back here in twenty minutes for the castle expedition," Tom said.

There was no question that our room had been a stall, and a minimum number of changes had been made to convert it into living quarters for two-legged animals. There was no closet or dresser, only large tacks on the wall that were probably once used for bridles and reins. The only light came from a single overhead bulb, the beds were camplike cots, and the towels that were provided were distinguished by their sandpaper quality. Of course there was no such luxury as a sink in our room: the nearest plumbing facility was five stalls away. But in spite of the primitive living conditions, we fell in love with Salsgate.

The opulence of the castle was overwhelming and it was easy to understand Mr. Gorley's pride. He imbued us with his enthusiasm for everything from the Versailles elegance of the mirrored ballroom and the lavishly decorated royal bedchambers, to the Queen's closet. At the end of his guided tour, he showed us the gardens of magnificent English roses, begonias, and delphiniums, an aquamarine pond with floating lily pads under a willow tree, and a vast lawn of rich green grass that covered at least an acre of land.

I was so immersed in the romantic medieval atmosphere that it came as a shock when some kids began playing Frisbee. My mental image of beautifully garbed princes and princesses romping on the green under the careful eye of a uniformed governess was shattered by the sight of an assorted bunch of teen-agers tossing plastic discs at each other.

It didn't seem to me that anyone could show off at such a simple game, but Sabrina was definitely making her presence felt. It was a warm day and I guess you could say she was dressed appropriately in short shorts and a sleeveless skin-tight t-shirt which happened to be red—literally a traffic-stopper. She made a special point of squealing with delight every time she caught or threw the Frisbee and I couldn't help noticing that Tom was her partner.

I've always felt slightly out of it when it comes to sports and since Frisbee didn't seem too demanding, I thought I might as well participate. There were at least half a dozen floating around, and when one landed at my feet I picked it up and whirled it toward Mike. He was standing closest to me, less than ten yards away, but the platter only made it half way and then fell to the ground. I ran to pick it up, but my sandal slipped on the grass and I found myself ungracefully sprawled on the ground. Mike hurried toward me and pulled me up. For a minute, I was too chagrined to even say thank you, and just stared at my sandals as though they had betrayed me. Finally, I assured Mike I was all in one piece, and he went off, saying, "Take it easy."

I decided I'd check out the lily pads and ambled over to the willow tree. On the way, I couldn't help noticing Tom and Sabrina laughing together. It occurred to me that they might be laughing at what a spaz I was, but I wasn't about to wait and find out. Instead, I dropped down under the tree with my back to them and tried not to feel sorry for myself. It was hard not to feel out of sync, especially when everyone else seemed to be *gamboling on the green,* and I was happily distracted when Peter stretched out beside me.

"Good place to meditate," he said. "What are you thinking?"

"I'm a Frisbee failure," I sighed. "Did you see me fall down?"

"I wondered if you hurt yourself?"

"Only my pride," I answered, and thought how easy it was to talk to Peter.

"I could give you a lesson," he volunteered.

"I rate zero on the athletic scale," I warned him.

"But I like challenges," he said, getting up and extending his hand to me.

"Promise not to laugh at me?"

"Never. And if you do what I say, I'll guarantee results."

Then he picked up the Frisbee he had brought with him, showed me how to hold it, stood behind me and covered my hand with his. "Bend zee wrist," he instructed, and after several practice swings he cried, "Let go!" and the Frisbee went flying more than thirty yards.

I was so excited that I jumped up and down, and then spontaneously hugged him. He hugged me back, and then to cover his unexpected spontaneous response and to hide his discomfiture, he insisted that I practice some more. He backed away, and I whirled the disc to him at least twenty more times with equal success.

"You're ready for the big leagues," Peter surmised, and I followed him toward the center of the green. I was no longer fearful of making a fool of myself and purposely planted myself near Tom so he could see me.

"You've been practicing," he observed, as Peter and I tossed the Frisbee back and forth. "When I first saw you, I thought you were a lost cause."

So why didn't you come to my rescue? I thought. But aloud I quipped, "Now I can play with the big boys."

"That's exactly what I was hoping. Perhaps after the concert tonight, you'll save some time for me—but not to play Frisbee."

"Why sure," I agreed.

"But now we'd better get ready to rehearse. I see Clyde and Julie are trying to round up the forces. And in case I don't get a chance to talk to you after the concert, meet me at ten o'clock under the moosehead in what looks like the king's study just off the Great Hall."

"I'll be there," I said, trying to keep the excitement out of my voice. I couldn't help being pleased that although he preferred playing games with Sabrina, it was me he wanted to see later. I couldn't wait.

Our supper of tasteless hamburger, canned peas, and soggy French fries was in sharp contrast to the baronial splendor of the dining hall where one huge oak table accommodated all of us, and royal ancestors looked down disapprovingly from the gilded frames that lined the walls. As always, there were a number of jokes about the food, but Mr. Saxe cleverly deflected the complaints, suggesting that jugged hare would be a more fitting dish. The idea of eating anything resembling a rabbit was enough to make us grateful for our American fare.

After changing into our concert mufti, we walked through the cobble-stoned streets of the village lined with thatched-roofed cottages to the stone church where our concert was to take place. In the back of the church, worn old stones marked the graves of parishioners who had died hundreds of years ago. It was mind-boggling to know that someone, perhaps exactly my age, had stood on the very same ground I was on and read in the sixteenth century the inscription on the tombstone:

Mary Cranmoor
1480–1517
May She Rest in Peace

I wanted to read all the tombstones and try to imagine what it would be like to have lived in another century. Ordinarily, in the States, the last thing I would do was to visit a cemetery, but in this quiet churchyard the idea of mortality seemed much more acceptable. With such cosmic thoughts, one would think I'd have a sense of proportion about Tom, but that wasn't the case at all. And although I loved the idea of singing in an ancient church, I couldn't wait until it was over and I could return to the castle.

On the way back, Daisy asked me if I wanted to join up with some kids who were going to a local pub.

"No thanks," I said without hesitation. "I'm meeting Tom."

"At least you're honest," she said, and skipped off.

It occurred to me as I entered the dimly lit castle that I had again rejected the opportunity to be part of the group, but I tried to put that out of my mind. It was eerie waiting for Tom under the somber eye of the moosehead and I had trouble keeping my mind off the possibility of ghosts. I was five minutes early and Tom was five minutes late, and by the time he had arrived I had worked myself into a state.

"You're here!" I shouted, as though I never expected to see him again.

"I'm a man of my word," he said smoothly, "unless unforeseen circumstances intervene."

"It's spooky around here alone," I told him.

"You're not alone anymore. As a matter of fact, I thought we'd investigate that winding stairway that Gorley pointed out. It's bound to lead somewhere."

"Sure," I agreed, not wanting to appear chicken.

He grabbed my hand and pulled me down the Great Hall to a dark passageway that led to curved stone stairs. Then Tom lit his gas pipe lighter so that we could see our way up the pitch black steps. The stairway was so narrow that we had to walk single file, but I was so afraid of losing Tom that I kept bumping into him, and giggled nervously.

"We're almost there," he said reassuringly, after what I considered an interminable climb.

I tried to keep in mind that exploring a medieval

castle was probably one of the most unique dates I'd ever have. However, the stairway was cold and dank, my legs were shaky, and I was half hoping that Tom would decide to give up this expedition when he stopped dead in front of a wooden door that was closed with an iron bolt.

"Hold this near the latch," he directed, handing me the lighter.

Then he slid the bolt to the side, and boldly stepped over the threshold. I followed gingerly behind and then gasped when I realized we were on the parapet of the castle, which was lit by a brilliant moon.

I'd always thought that moonlight was just something people wrote about in love songs, but now I understood why.

"Worth the trip?" Tom asked, putting his arm around me.

"It's beautiful," I whispered, taking in the view of the village and the surrounding countryside.

"And I think you're beautiful," Tom uttered, as he turned to face me. He put his other hand around my waist and pressed me to him as he covered my mouth with his lips. We stayed locked together for a long time.

I wanted that kiss to go on forever, but I knew it was up to me to break away. Tom would think less of me if I let him go on, and I gently pushed him off. The temperature had dropped and I was beginning to tremble, which gave me a good excuse.

"We better go back," I said breathlessly. "I'm beginning to freeze."

"Whatever you say, darling."

I was a little disappointed that he didn't give me an argument, but then it was late, and he must have been cold, too.

I floated downstairs as though I were in a dream. I

was still in a daze when we retraced our steps through the Great Hall to the door of the castle. On the way to the "stable" we passed several groups of kids who were walking around the grounds, and Tom again was the efficient courier, not even holding my hand. When he dropped me off at my stall, he didn't even give me a goodnight peck on the cheek, but I understood perfectly.

Daisy hadn't come in yet, and I was grateful that I didn't have to make conversation. I wanted to be alone with my thoughts, to recall in minute detail our romantic interlude. Tom, Tom, Tom was all I could think when I finally fell into a deep dreamless sleep.

The remaining days at Salsgate Tom and I were never alone. I tried to convince myself it was because of the lack of opportunity, the demands of his job, and our heavy concert schedule. There were concerts planned for every evening in parishes located quite a distance away, and that meant getting back late. I was sure he hadn't forgotten what I romantically thought of as our tryst, because he occasionally gave me one of his penetrating looks, or would press my arm meaningfully when he passed by. And I didn't see him paying special attention to anyone else, not even Sabrina, so I believed our separation was a result of external circumstance.

I just knew things would change when we got to Yorkshire, our next stop. Evan cornered me at breakfast our last day at Salsgate and provided me with an encyclopedic description of the North country. His observations on the rock formations, and the unique quality of the Yorkshire region made me remember *Wuthering Heights*. The rugged moors perfectly suited the passionate nature of Heathcliff—my Tom—and I, of course, was his adored Catherine. My imagination conjured up a vision of Tom and me, strolling on the heath, perhaps buffeted by the wind, and then embracing each other for protection from the elemental forces of nature.

"For the third time, Beth, am I boring you?" Evan shouted at me.

"What? No, no, not at all," I replied, realizing that his droning on had lulled me into a private reverie.

"You had such a faraway look in your eyes, I couldn't tell if you were still listening."

"Course I was. Sounds terrific." I tried to sound as bright as possible.

Then, before he could start asking questions, I told him I'd heard that we were going to stop at a flea market along the way. "Julie said it would break up the trip as well as provide local color. We're almost halfway through, and I still haven't bought my parents anything."

"I'm sure you'll find something. This part of England has some excellent antique fairs, and the prices are far more reasonable than anything you'd find in London. However, with the value of the dollar down, and the inflation rate rising . . ."

"I've really got to go and finish some last minute things," I said getting up from the table. I didn't want to be rude, but I wasn't ready for an analysis of the English monetary system.

"See ya," he called, as I rushed off purposefully.

Actually, I had finished all my packing, but I wanted to make one quick tour of the castle and grounds. There wasn't time to climb what I now thought of as Tom's and my secret staircase, but I could make a last quick inspection of the Great Hall, the Gold Room, and the ballroom. I ended up in the king's study and defiantly peered at the moosehead that seemed much less fearsome in daylight. I shut my eyes and for the zillionth time I lived through every moment of my assignation with Tom. When I heard footsteps entering the room, I quickly turned around hoping no one had seen me in such a silly attitude.

"Paying homage to the moosehead?" To my enormous relief it was Peter, who never made me uncomfortable even when he teased.

"Trying to stare him down. At night, he looks a lot more alive and ferocious."

"That's funny. That's just what Sabrina was saying at breakfast."

"How would she know?" I asked sharply.

"I was only half-listening, but something about how she was sure the moose blinked at her while she awaited her knight in shining armor."

"Her knight in shining armor," I repeated. I knew that could only be Tom. There's no one else that Sabrina would refer to that way, and I just had to know more no matter how painful.

"Well," I said lightly, trying to disguise the heaviness of my heart, "I suppose she was whisked off on his white horse."

"Something like that," Peter said, giving me a funny look. "She said she found herself on the top of the castle that commanded a view for miles."

"And then?"

"And then, I don't know. She was still going on, embellishing her role as heroine in her little drama, when I finally broke away."

"I see," I muttered, and swiftly turned to inspect the giltwood mantel over the fireplace. Not that I was all that interested in the intricate carving, but I needed a minute to compose myself.

"Anyway, let's take one last look at the lily pond," Peter urged.

"Let's," I agreed, suddenly realizing that I couldn't wait to leave what just minutes before I had considered Tom's and my place.

Fortunately, Peter didn't feel like talking as we strolled toward the pond and I tried to sort out my thoughts. If Tom didn't really like me, then why bother with me at all? I'd been flattered—mistakenly so—that he'd risk breaking the courier rules just for me. It's obvious he'd break them for anybody. But what was his game? It was hard to know, but I sensed that Peter had been trying to warn me. Or was that my overactive imagination?

We had arrived at the edge of the pond, as cool and still as blue crystal, which was exactly the opposite of how I felt. I recalled one of Ms. Bevins's crazy assignments: to keep a diary on the effects of nature on mood. Everyone in the class, including me, came to the conclusion that our mental state was definitely affected by the elements. But as I gazed at the tranquil water, I thought I'd have to revise that conclusion. I couldn't ever remember being so out of tune with my environment.

"You look awfully serious," Peter observed.

It was a relief to have my inner dialogue interrupted and I told him about the Bevin assignment and the conclusions we'd drawn.

"You were younger then," he joked. Then, as if he knew I was having a granddaddy of downers, he added, "I bet once you see the wild moors of Yorkshire, you'll feel as serene as this lake."

I half-smiled at his imagery. "You're a poet as well as a musician."

"Sure," he muttered.

I didn't think I'd said anything terribly personal or praised him excessively, but a telltale crimson mark showed on his face. "You're funny," I said spontaneously, for the moment not thinking about myself. "You're the most secure performer here, but you seem to die if anyone says anything personal about you, even if it's a compliment."

"Not anyone," he corrected.

I looked at him hard, but before I could ask him to explain further, he grabbed my arm and pulled me back from the edge of the pond. "We've got to go," he said pointedly. "Where will the Bryant choir be without its two star performers?"

"In a lot of trouble," I answered, and then I really was smiling.

On the bus ride, as usual, there was a combination of singing, shouting and six-way conversations. The "transfers," which is what Tom called the process of going from one place to another, I considered a form of therapy. Not only could you do your own thing—everything from knitting to writing letters to reading—but you could choose to do nothing. The latter was for me, and I found a seat by myself in the back of the bus where I tried to get my head together.

The morning wasn't half over, and already I had experienced a bittersweet farewell with moosehead; a disturbing view of Tom; and a new feeling for Peter that I couldn't quite fathom. Again, I found myself in the position of talking myself out of Tom. If I could just stop thinking about him, my problems would be solved. I was so involved in my own thoughts that I actually had to shake my head to bring myself back to the present when the bus lurched to a stop in a car-park.

Tom had picked up the microphone and was making an announcement. He looked more handsome than ever, having picked up a tan that gave him a bronze complexion and highlighted his hair. He was wearing a light-blue cotton shirt that made his eyes even more intensely blue.

"Here we are, choir, at Scarborough," he began. "Home of the famed Scarborough fair. A bit different from the days of the Renaissance, but there happens to be a flea market in session. With a little imagination you can transport yourself back to the sixteenth century."

How could I put him out of my mind when everything about him was so incredible?

"I'll lead you directly to the flea market," he continued. "Be back on the bus in one hour, and we'll make the final leg of the trip to York. Lunch is independent, and I suggest you fuel up on some meat pasties or pizza which are modern Scarborough specialities."

I hurried off the bus with the others and we all followed Tom for several blocks through this bustling seaside resort to an open flea market. Since we only had one hour, and I was intent on finding something for my parents, I hopped from booth to booth, not paying any attention to any of the other kids. Each proprietor specialized in a particular kind of item—glassware, silver, snuff boxes, candlesticks, old books, even antique lace. There were so many possibilities that I despaired of ever making the right choice. Then I came upon an old sampler that depicted a one-story cottage surrounded by tiny flowers. Woven into the pattern was the line: SUSAN—SEVEN YEARS OLD—1892. It was the perfect present for my mother who I knew would hang it in her needlepoint shop.

In spite of my volunteering to take it in tissue paper, the bespectacled frail little lady who waited on me insisted, once she heard I was buying it for my mother, to wrap the sampler in gift paper. That was a much longer procedure than it should have been, because the poor lady had arthritic fingers, and after slowly wrapping my gift in exquisite violet-embossed paper, she painfully tied it with an elaborate bow. I paid her the exact amount in order to avoid a further delay, thanked her profusely for her efforts, and rushed off.

There were only twenty minutes left and I almost gave up on finding my father anything appropriate until I discovered a smoking booth. I selected what appeared to be an authentic seaman's meerschaum pipe. I had to have it, and told the scraggly bearded weather-beaten proprietor, who was wearing a sailor's cap, that I would take it as is. He held it up admiringly and told me the pipe had a history that he must share with me.

"This pipe," he said, stroking it fondly, "was owned by a U-boat captain captured during the Second World War. The British Navy forced the captain to give up his possessions, and this was among his personal belongings."

"That's fascinating," I remarked, knowing I'd just heard a romantic bit of fiction. Then I paid him two pounds, plunked the pipe that he reluctantly handed to me into my bag, and backed away quickly before he could regale me with any more tales. I glanced at my watch and saw that I had ten minutes to reach the bus. I started off in what I thought was the right direction, but nothing seemed familiar. Then, to my horror, I realized that I had lost my bearings.

I looked around frantically for someone from our group, but I couldn't find one familiar face. Then, remembering my mother's telling me when I was very young that if I ever got lost to ask a policeman what to do, I approached a bobby. He looked a little forbidding in his dark blue uniform and imposing tall rounded hat as he strutted among the crowd, but I had no other choice but to ask for his help.

"Officer," I began, "can you tell me where the car-park is located? I have to get back to our bus, and I don't know which way to go." I tried to keep the panic out of my voice, and I must have succeeded too well because the bobby cleared his throat, stroked his chin, and then peered at me under his beetle brows for at least a minute before speaking.

"American, aren't you, missy?" he asked.

"Yes," I replied, praying he wouldn't waste time making conversation.

"Well, there are two possibilities—two parking areas, that is. One's south and one's north. Which way did you come from?"

"From Salsgate," I said, not trusting myself to give the right direction.

"Beautiful castle up there, huh?"

"Yes, but please tell me. I'm late and they'll all be waiting and Mr. Saxe will be furious." I saw that I was already overdue and started to blubber uncontrollably.

"There, there, missy. You mustn't carry on so. My guess is that you came from a northerly direction and therefore your bus is out there, three blocks to your left."

Though my eyes were blurred with tears, I could see where he was pointing and after mumbling thank you, I fled. Once I was out of the marketplace, I recognized the route we had come, and tore down the blocks to the bus. I managed to stop crying, but I had crushed the delicate wrapping on my mother's present and the artfully tied bow had fallen off by the time I reached the bus. But that was the least of my worries.

From nearly a block away I could see that Mr. Saxe was fuming. He and Joe, our burly, good-natured driver, were pacing up and down. Everyone else was obviously inside. I felt totally wrecked from the marathon I'd just run, and the combination of fear and physical exertion must have drained the blood from my cheeks. I was expecting Mr. Saxe to explode in rage. Instead, probably because I looked so disheveled and miserable, his face unexpectedly softened.

"Better sit down, Beth. You look like you've had it."

I smiled wanly, enormously grateful that he hadn't attacked me verbally, and climbed into the bus where the silence was oppressive.

"I'm sorry, I'm sorry," I murmured, as I made my way to a seat in the back. I was still somewhat dazed, but not so out of it that I didn't hear several remarks which weren't all entirely comforting.

"She gets away with it because she's his pet."

"Yeah, anyone else, and they'd get Saxe's 'tyranny of the individual' routine."

"Thinks she's a privileged person just because she happens to have the best voice."

"Maybe she has an explanation."

"That's right, anyone can get lost."

"Notice she was too snobby to stick with anyone, had to go off on her own."

"Maybe she had a reason."

I slunk down into an empty seat and kept my head down, hoping to blot out any more opinions. As the bus picked up speed, someone started singing "Scarborough Fair" and soon everyone had joined in.

I never felt so horrible in my life and didn't blame anyone for being mad at me. I had always been a nut about everyone else being on time, and never was very understanding about their excuses. Maybe I was learning to be tolerant the hard way.

Then, when I thought that I'd never feel good again, someone plopped down on the seat next to me.

"You're only human." It was a familiar girl's voice and I couldn't believe my ears. I looked up slowly, thinking this was all a dream, and then the tears streamed down my face.

"Patsy," I cried incoherently, "Patsy." More than anything in the world I needed a friend, someone to reach out to me, and she knew it.

"You've mutilated that present, Beth," she said, taking the battered gift box from my lap. "Fortunately, I have some pastel tissue paper which my mother thought might come in handy. Perfect for wrapping presents. Can I look at what you bought?"

"You can do anything," I murmured, wondering if I lived to be a hundred if I could ever repay her.

8

The next few days were relatively calm in what I was beginning to view as my roller-coaster existence. I hadn't realized how much I'd missed Patsy, and knowing she was still my friend filled an enormous gap. Since we hadn't spoken to each other for a while, it came as a surprise when she confided to me that she really liked Timmy.

"He's really cute," I said.

"But a little dense when it comes to women," she groaned.

We were in Daisy's and my room after our first concert in York, which took place at the guild hall.

Daisy was lying on her bed, mooning over a letter from Greg that she had just received, and tore herself away from reading it for the zillionth time to say, "You can change all that."

"I'm trying, I'm trying," Patsy stated, "but I'm not sure he really knows the difference between boys and

116

girls—except that boys are tenors and basses and girls are altos and sopranos."

Then we had one of our old-time giggling fits and when we recovered, Patsy brought out her trusty guidebook. "Tomorrow we have a free afternoon, and I think we should make a walking tour of York. It's an honest-to-goodness walled city, and it says here we can 'walk the medieval town walls.' Then we'll wind up at the cathedral which, according to this, 'boasts some of England's finest stained glass.'"

That night when I went to sleep I thought how lucky I was that some of the crises in my life were getting solved. No one had mentioned the flea market episode since our arrival in York, and I assumed that I'd been forgiven by the other members of the choir. They must have known how genuinely contrite I was, and I attributed a lot of their unkind remarks to the fact that they were impatient, hot, and restless waiting in the stuffy bus where the air conditioning only worked when the bus was moving. But I learned the next morning that that was a false assumption.

We were having a rehearsal in the main sitting room of the Victorian hotel where we were staying. I was doing a small soprano solo that was a recitative of a Bach cantata and had just stepped forward to begin singing when Tom came charging into the room. He apologized to everyone for interrupting, and then told Mr. Saxe he was wanted on the phone.

"It's London calling," he explained. "They must talk to you about arrangements for our final concert at the Rivers Parish Church."

"I guess that can't wait," Mr. Saxe grumbled. Then, probably just because I was standing next to him, he handed me the baton and said, "Take over, Beth. I'll be back as soon as possible."

I was in a state of shock but automatically walked to the front of the music stand and faced the chorus. "Okay, everybody, let's take it from the top."

As I lifted my hand to give them a downbeat, a deep voice boomed from the back row, "Top of what?"

"Yeah, what if you're topless, like me?" someone else squeaked.

"Better than being bottomless," another chimed in.

"Please," I implored, "let's try to work on something while Mr. Saxe is gone."

"We are. We're working on topping each other."

I felt caught in a maze and didn't know whether to laugh or cry. Mr. Saxe had been gone for less than five minutes, and already there was bedlam.

"Please," I started again, hoping to get their attention, but there was so much noise, no one could hear me. Then suddenly, like a thunderclap, three loud chords were heard from the piano, and for an instant everyone stopped talking.

Peter took advantage of the momentary silence to make what amounted to an impassioned plea. "Look," he intoned softly, "we didn't work this long and this hard and travel this distance to behave like a bunch of idiots. If we're not serious about why we're here, we might as well forget about performing and spend the rest of the tour living it up."

Everyone was startled by the fact that Peter had spoken up. He always seemed to blend into the crowd, and never made waves. Yet, in his quiet way, he had captured the group's attention. There was a stunned silence followed by a low murmur of voices, but this time they were no longer wisecracking. Remarks like, "he's right, you know"; "we've gotten such great reactions, we'd be crazy to blow it now"; and "we really shouldn't waste time" filled the room.

Then Peter looked at me and nodded his head which I took as my cue to continue. It took every ounce of my courage, because I had no assurance that they wouldn't make fun of me again, and trying to keep the waver out of my voice, I said, "Let's take it from the top."

This time when I gave them a downbeat, they responded seriously, and when Mr. Saxe returned almost ten minutes later he never could have guessed the difficulty I had at first.

He was listening during the last few minutes and when I gave them the final cutoff, Mr. Saxe said, "Not bad at all, Beth. If I knew you were going to be a threat to my career, I would never have left the room."

I knew he was being funny, but I couldn't help being delighted. It did bother me, though, that except for a few titters, the choir as a whole didn't seem too pleased.

When rehearsal was over, Peter remained seated at the piano, scribbling some notes on his sheet music. I waited until everyone had gone, and then slid next to him on the piano bench.

"You saved my life, Peter. I honestly thought I was going to die when they started acting up."

"Everyone listens to the piano. It's my secret weapon." As always, Peter was being modest.

"They sure weren't going to listen to me," I groaned. "Do you realize, this is the second time you've come to my rescue?"

"Teaching you how to play Frisbee wasn't exactly a life-saving procedure."

"I thought it was. You changed my life."

I was half-kidding but he looked at me very seriously. "I picked something up at the flea market for you and I've been waiting for a chance to give it to you."

"For me?"

He pulled a small package out of his jacket pocket and handed it to me. "Breakable," he warned.

I opened it carefully and when I saw the contents I didn't know whether to take it seriously. It was an exact replica of the Discus Thrower, the classical Greek sculpture.

"It's terrific," I exclaimed, finally.

"You really like it?"

"I love it. It'll always remind me of the day I mastered that plastic platter."

"And me, too, I hope."

"The day I mastered you?"

"No," he protested, his face flushed, "it'll remind you of me, I hope."

"Oh, of course. If it weren't for you, I'd never have been prepared for the Olympics."

We were both laughing when Patsy stuck her head in the door and shouted that her walking tour was going to begin promptly after lunch. "Which is now being served," she said, before disappearing.

"Why don't you come too, Peter?" I asked. "We're literally going to climb the walls."

"I'd love to," Peter replied, "but I have got to spend some time practicing."

"I know how it is," I sympathized, sliding off the bench. "But we both better get some chow now, or we'll be out of luck."

"You're right," he said, following me.

Then I suddenly stopped short and I turned to face him. Before I thought through what effect it would have on him, I kissed him quickly on the cheek and murmured, "thank you," in his ear.

"Thank you," he muttered, "I . . . I only . . ."

But before he could finish his sentence, I turned and headed for the door. "Beth, come back," I heard him say, but I was too surprised at my own behavior to wait and maybe have to offer any explanation. I hurried into the dining room and took a seat at a table with Patsy and Daisy.

"You look flustered," Patsy remarked.

"Just rushing," I said, not sure myself why I had run away from Peter. It was only a sisterly kiss, hardly a commitment. And I felt nothing like I did when Tom had embraced me. And yet . . .

Walking the walls was an unusual, if somewhat chilling, experience. In some places, there was a drop of more than twenty-five feet, the wall narrowed to less than a foot wide, and with no guard rails, sudden death seemed quite possible. However, I followed along bravely, trying to enjoy the sights of ancient ruins, meandering streets overhung with gables of shops and houses, and charming courtyards. At the end of our walk I felt I had accomplished an acrobatic feat and Patsy's directive that we were going to climb to the top of Minster's bell tower seemed like kid stuff.

First, we inspected the magnificent interior of the cathedral and then assembled at the bottom of the bell tower where several other members of our choir were about to embark on this excursion. We greeted each other like long-lost friends, even though we'd been separated for less than an hour. I tried not to let it bother me that Tom and Sabrina were part of the other group. After all, that might have been coincidence, and now we were all joining forces.

A sign at the bottom of the first step warned that the climb was not recommended for anyone with heart problems. I had plenty of heart problems, I thought, but not the kind that would be affected by five-hundred steps.

Clyde offered to lead the way, promising to keep a slow but steady pace. "No point in hurrying. I understand that midway there's a catwalk where we can take a breather and the faint-hearted can retrace their steps."

The way he phrased the possibility that some of us might back down was a challenge and made me more determined than ever to make it to the top.

Clyde started out and we fell in behind him, gaggling away in our usual manner. However, after the first hundred steps our conversation dwindled to an occasional "Who's idea was this?" and "Will this ever end?" Finally, all that could be heard was heavy huffing and puffing.

It was a relief to reach the catwalk after the claustrophobic stairway, but it held its own terrors—a precariously narrow twenty-foot passageway lined with guardrails. Standing on the catwalk, we were level with the flying buttresses and gargoyles; this gave us the eerie sensation that we were an extension of the cathedral.

"Everyone okay?" Clyde asked, once we had all emerged.

I found the combination of light, height, and fresh air dizzying, but I wasn't about to admit it and be called chicken.

"We're all fine," someone called out behind me.

"Not all," I heard Tom say.

I turned around and saw that Sabrina was leaning against Tom, practically in a swoon.

"Oh, oh," Clyde said, squeezing past me to where they were standing. "What's wrong, Sabrina?"

"Vertigo," she replied weakly, as though she were a Victorian princess suffering from the vapors.

"I'll take care of her," Tom volunteered promptly. "You take the others to the top and we'll wend our way back down."

"Oh, Tom," she whined, "I hate to hold you back."

"No problem. I've been to the bell tower many times."

"You're sure?"

"Of course I'm sure."

I didn't know if she was faking or not, but I suddenly wondered why I was so anxious to be a good sport. It didn't accomplish anything, I was feeling queasy and couldn't complain about it, and because of my misguided bravery, I had thrust Tom into the arms of another woman.

My adrenalin was working overtime as we made the final flight of steps. The view was breathtaking and we could see for miles beyond the city of York to the valleys and moors of Bronte country. For the moment, at least, I felt how insignificant my problems were in comparison to the vast beauty of Yorkshire. However, my philosophical attitude didn't last for long when the image of Sabrina and Tom kept returning to dominate my befuddled head.

As we trudged down the stairs, my case of "spiralitis" became more acute. I think everyone was suffering to some extent, and tried to make jokes about mountain climbers getting severe frostbite and losing more toes descending than ascending. Such remarks did little to bolster my spirits, and I didn't think the labyrinth winding would ever end. Not only was my head spinning, but my knees were beginning to feel weak.

It took several minutes for me to catch my breath, regain my balance, and adjust to the glaring sunlight once I'd finished negotiating the last steps. I collapsed on the lawn, along with all the others, who seemed to be experiencing the same reentry problems. When I was able to focus my eyes, I saw Sabrina leaning against a boulder, Tom hovering over her. She looked perfectly relaxed and healthy, and then Tom handed her an ice cream cone which she accepted, smiling beguilingly.

Tom's back was to me, so I couldn't see what he was saying, but the next thing I knew he walked over to us and solicitously asked us about our well being.

"It was a little hairy in spots, but I think we've all recovered," Clyde said, looking around. "How's Sabrina?"

"Perfect," Tom replied, and I trusted he was referring to her health.

"I think we should take it easy the rest of the afternoon, because we have dinner at six, then a concert," Clyde suggested.

"Good idea," Tom said. "And after the concert the hotel is letting us take over their disco room, which is more like a cellar with a juke box and tables and a patch of wooden floor that serves as a dance area."

"Let's get going, gang," Julie said. "Too much sun after that climb in the dark might scramble our brains."

We dragged ourselves up and slowly headed for the hotel. Patsy whispered to me, "I'm really looking forward to the party, assuming I can get Timmy to dance."

"Sure you will," I said, aware that I had been thinking the same thing, with a different cast of characters, that is, if I could get Tom to dance with me.

I was still feeling a little weak, but didn't want to let on. Therefore, I was amazed when Tom came up to me and said, "You look a little pale, Beth. Are you sure you're okay?"

"Perfect," I replied, echoing his description of Sabrina. And again I wondered why I couldn't answer the simplest question from Tom without making a fool of myself.

9

The idea of a party turned us all on. We'd seen each other under all sorts of circumstances and in some of the most trying conditions and we were looking forward to just having fun. We returned to the hotel after the concert to change clothes. Nobody wanted to make a big deal of dressing up and the girls mutually agreed to wear jeans. But I broke out my favorite pink angora sweater that I'd been saving, and I noticed that everyone else made an effort to look special.

The disco was exactly as Tom had described it—a converted cellar. There were Japanese lanterns that covered the original bare bulbs hanging from the ceiling; music blasted from the juke box; plastic-covered tables surrounded a barely adequate dance floor. And yet, in spite of the unglamorous setting, there was a festive atmosphere that everyone seemed to share.

When Daisy and I made our way downstairs to the

cellar, I vaguely wondered why going to a party, even one as informal as this, was exciting. Maybe it was because people act different at parties, and the unexpected always happens. Otherwise, why are some parties good and some bad, even though the guests are the same?

Of course, I had steeled myself for the possibility that Tom wouldn't pay attention to me. This was such an obvious place for him to show favoritism that he'd probably bend over backwards to be fair. Therefore, I was astounded when I entered the room, which was already half filled, and before I could get accustomed to the dim light, was grabbed by the arm and pulled onto the dance floor by Tom.

"I've been waiting for you. What took you so long?" he asked in a low voice.

I hoped he didn't expect a sensible response, because I was too conscious of his arms around me, his body pressed to mine. I closed my eyes and for a few seconds imagined we were gliding along the dance floor of a gilded ballroom instead of being crushed in this made-over basement. Then, in keeping with my reverie, he whispered in my ear, "You look sensational in pink."

"You do, too," I said without thinking.

"Sensational in pink?" he chuckled.

"Just sensational," I explained, surprised at my boldness.

"You're also a fantastic dancer," he went on.

"Fantastic," I echoed.

"This conversation isn't going anywhere, but I love it," he said.

"Love it."

"Perhaps we can continue it later. There's a lovely park near here and I'd like to show it to you. Game?"

"Sure, I'm game."

We were dancing to a Johnny Mathis song and I wanted it to go on all night. Johnny Mathis sang ballads in a low husky voice, and in my mesmerized state I believed that as long as the record kept playing, I would have Tom to myself. But as soon as the music ended, my enraptured moment with Tom was dramatically interrupted. Someone had selected a new-wave hit that blared out from the juke box and precluded holding one's partner. I found myself facing Evan, who was gyrating awkwardly. Presumably, he was dancing with me. Tom mumbled something in my ear about "the park, later," and then disappeared into the crowd. I tried to coordinate my dancing, separate but equal, with Evan's, but since touching each other was never required, it really didn't matter. To my relief, he quickly became disenchanted and suggested we check out the refreshment table.

He ran interference for me to the far end of the room where there was a table offering the English equivalent of junk food:—crisps, crocks of cheese, water biscuits, and a dubious-looking punch consisting of fizzy water and sherbet. Evan piled a paper plate with some food, I carried two glasses of punch, and we settled at a table where Clyde, Julie, and Mr. Saxe happened to be sitting.

I was completely distracted, thinking about Tom and wondering if we could get together later without being discovered. I also hoped he would ask me to dance again. I couldn't ever remember being so perfectly synchronized with someone on the dance floor.

"Hey, Beth," Mr. Saxe roared, "how about showing me how it's done?"

"Who, me?" I answered, taken off guard.

"He's only been asking you for five minutes," Clyde said, chuckling.

"Oh, I'm sorry," I apologized. "I was thinking about something."

"Obviously," Mr. Saxe remarked, and gave me such a probing look as if I was sure he could read my mind. Then, he added, "We better get out there now while they're playing something that remotely resembles dance music."

"That's the Police's version of "Roxanne," I explained, as I followed him to the floor.

Saxe was definitely a square when it came to dancing and I wasn't sure why he'd asked me, although I was flattered. Then he said something about English rock groups and I tried to listen although the decibel count made it difficult to hear.

"Some of them are original and have real substance, like the Beatles," he was saying.

"Uh huh," I muttered, and nodded my head, more intent on not letting him step on my feet than in a musical discussion.

"Others are superficially appealing, but not trustworthy."

"Yes," I agreed, still somewhat baffled as to why he would choose this time and place to talk about rock bands.

"Just like some Englishmen I know," he said.

"I only know one Englishman," I began, "and he's . . ." I stopped abruptly. Was Mr. Saxe trying to tell me something about Tom? Or was I so besotted with my feelings for him, that whatever anyone talked about I immediately interpreted in terms of Tom. I knew Saxe rarely made personal remarks, but I couldn't help thinking that his analogy between English rock groups and Englishmen was more than an oblique reference to Tom. There was no way he knew I planned to meet Tom later. What was he getting at? Were my emotions so transparent that he thought I might get hurt?

I was tempted to ask him directly, but something held me back. I really didn't want to know the answers. Then the record was over and Kiki edged herself between us. I might have considered that the height of rudeness from anyone else, but it was the kind of thing one expected from Kiki. Besides, I was grateful for a chance to escape from any more insinuations about Tom.

"Me, next," Kiki was saying as I backed off.

I wasn't looking where I was going and crashed into someone.

"Oh, I'm sorry," I shouted, and turned around to see Peter grinning at me.

"Not your fault," he said. "I planned it that way—hoping to corner you before you got away."

He drew me to him, obviously anticipating a slow number, but then a wild punk sound blasted us and everyone started doing the pogo, hardly a romantic dance since it meant leaping up and down in the air like Mexican jumping beans. After a few minutes, we both bogged down and Peter suggested we go for a walk. Ordinarily, I might have been agreeable to the idea, but I didn't want to mess up my chance of a rendezvous with Tom. I hesitated so long, trying to think up an excuse, that Peter finally said, "I guess you don't want to."

"It's not that, it's just that . . ."

"Never mind," he said, quickly.

We were still standing on the dance floor, surrounded by bodies energetically "pogoing" while we carried on this half-baked conversation. Then I noticed Tom giving me the hi sign, holding up five fingers, and pointing toward the door. If I read him correctly, that meant I should prepare to exit in five minutes.

Peter was facing me and therefore, couldn't see Tom signaling me. I had to pull a disappearing act without arousing suspicions. I figured the best way was to make an excuse about going to the "loo," which is what the ladies' lounge is called in England. It was located upstairs off the lobby, and after five minutes, I would cautiously drift outside.

"Before we get clobbered, we better move," Peter suggested, and deftly maneuvered himself off the floor. I followed close behind but before he could suggest sitting somewhere, I told him I was going to make a trip upstairs.

"Later," I said, as I moved away.

"See ya," Peter called back, and headed for a table where Priscilla was sitting. For a second, I was inexplicably torn—I didn't want Peter paying attention to anyone else. But that was ridiculous, since it was Tom I wanted more than anything in the world.

When I got upstairs I did go to the loo and killed the next few minutes combing my hair. Before I stepped into the lobby, I looked around furtively to make sure I wasn't seen and then headed for the exit to the street.

It was cool and breezy on the portico where I waited for Tom and I shivered from the night air as well as with the delicious prospect of our secret meeting. Tom appeared almost immediately, silently took my hand, and hurriedly led me away.

"I should have brought a jacket," I whispered, when we were a safe distance from the hotel.

"I'll keep you warm," he laughed, putting his arm around me.

The park, only a couple of blocks away, was dimly lit

by street lamps widely spaced along the pathways. Once my eyes became accustomed to the dark, I could see that flowerbeds dotted the manicured lawns, and benches had been strategically placed beneath the imposing trees.

"This is beautiful," I said.

"Even more so with you here," Tom said, and guided me toward a bench. Except for several other couples who had also discovered Tom's park, the place was deserted.

It really was cold, but I didn't want to spoil anything by complaining. Tom wrapped his arms around me and kissed me with what I thought was experienced technique. As he slowly slid his hand down from the back of my head to my waist, I felt tingles to the bottom of my feet which made me forget about the weather, and everything else for that matter. Therefore, it came as a shock when I heard a familiar voice say, "Looks like these English parks are getting more interesting by the minute."

Tom and I abruptly pulled away from each other in time to see Patsy and Timmy strolling by, hand-in-hand.

"Oh, oh," I sighed. "We've been discovered."

"That was Patsy and Timmy. They're probably just as anxious to be by themselves as we are."

"I know, but there may be others coming along and I didn't think it was a good idea for you to be seen with anyone."

"Don't worry your little head, darling." He started to kiss me again, but I suddenly felt very self-conscious and he could feel my resistance.

"I'm sorry, but things could get very sticky if the wrong person should see us."

"Well, if you're not willing to take risks . . ." He removed his arms from my shoulders, leaned back against the bench, and stared at the starry sky.

"Please understand, Tom. I'm just trying to protect you." I hated myself for sounding like a mother hen.

He had dropped his head down, and his arms hung between his knees in the most forlorn way. I knew the best way to kill romance was to act like a goody-goody, and that was exactly what I had done. Therefore I was amazed when Tom said, "I know, Beth. But with you, I just get carried away."

I wasn't quite sure if he meant that, but then he added, "Next week, when we're closer to the end of the tour and we're back in London, we can be a little more devil-may-care."

"You really do want to see me," I exclaimed, unable to disguise my misgivings.

"Of course, I do, Beth, and I wasn't kidding about coming to visit you."

"Oh, Tom," I sighed, "that would be so wonderful. But you've got to be prepared—suburban Cleveland isn't nearly as exciting as London."

"It will be if you're there," he avowed so sincerely that any doubts I had about him vanished.

As our bus tooled along on the way to London, I half dozed. In my semi-conscious state, I thought how much we'd packed into a couple of weeks. I, personally, was exhausted, not just from the demands of a heavy concert schedule and wanting to absorb as much of the local color as possible, but because of the emotional energy I'd expended. I hadn't for a minute forgotten Tom's saying that once we were back in London, we could be a little more "devil-may-care."

He never did elaborate on that statement, but I'd primed myself to agree to do whatever he wanted. With that pleasing thought, I fell sound asleep.

The next thing I knew, I was jolted awake by an ear-piercing screeching of brakes, a violent careening of the bus to the side of the road, and hysterical voices shouting, "What's happened?" "Did you see that guy take off?" "We could have been killed!"

I was sitting next to the window on the left side and could see that the bus had ground to a halt on an inclined curve. The back half of the bus was jutting out on the narrow road and the front was precariously hung over a soft drop. Mr. Saxe had grabbed the microphone, and although he tried to appear cool, his voice betrayed him. "Is everyone okay?" he asked. "Look around and see that your neighbor is in one piece." Then he handed the mike to Tom and I could see that he was shaken.

Tom implored everyone to remain seated while Julie and Clyde went up and down the aisle, checking on our condition. Then Clyde reported that it would take more than a swerving bus to upset such a hearty bunch, and we all applauded.

"Thanks to Joe's spectacular reflexes," Tom said, "we're very much alive. That sports car he managed to avoid must have been practicing for Le Mans."

"Let's hear it for Joe!" Mr. Saxe shouted, looking slightly less ashen, and we all hooted and hollered our appreciation.

Joe, who was still steaming from the near miss, growled, "I'd like to get my hands on that bloody driver."

That remark set us off again, and we yelled like a bunch of raving lunatics. Finally, Tom pleaded with us to calm down, so that he could tell us what was happening.

"It's essential for us to get towed out of this mess, which means Clyde and Joe will go for help. Joe says there's a village less than a kilometer away where he can call the bus company that will send a tow truck. Meanwhile, we'll need forces to wave traffic around the bus so that we don't get clobbered. Any volunteers?"

I immediately raised my hand. I'd felt totally wrecked before the accident, but now I was wide awake and eager to help. So was everyone else, I noticed, with the exception of Sabrina, who was sitting in front of me, rubbing the back of her neck, and complaining about whiplash. "I think I might have pulled a muscle," she whimpered to Tom as he came down the aisle to indicate who we would be paired with and where we would position ourselves. He looked at her sympathetically, then turned to me.

"You and Daisy will be at the bottom of the hill in the fourth group, right after Peter and Priscilla. You'll stay on duty fifteen minutes and then you'll be relieved. Let's hope the tow truck comes before the clouds break. It looks very threatening."

I was looking forward to getting off the bus, and actually I considered the whole incident something of a lark since none of us was hurt, but I had a visceral reaction when Tom mentioned that Priscilla and Peter were partners. Was that just coincidence, or had Priscilla—or Peter—planned it that way? Then I observed that they had been sitting together the whole trip, and that Peter hadn't made any attempt to see how I'd survived. But then, why should he? I had no claims on him just because he'd always been there when I needed him, like an old shoe. Still, I would have thought he'd want to know first-hand if I'd suffered any ill effects.

I was thinking about this so hard that I wasn't prepared for Patsy, who had bounded up the aisle to where I was sitting.

"Hey, don't look so glum, Beth. We'll be out of here soon, you know."

"I know," I muttered.

"What's the matter, then? I think this whole thing has cosmic qualities. Timmy and I have been cracking up over the idea of playing traffic cop."

"It will be fun." I tried to fake enthusiasm.

"See ya later," she said, skipping off.

Someone had started the song that goes, "You'll take the high road and I'll take the low," and I tried to get in the spirit of things and halfheartedly joined in the singing. The more I thought about it, the less appealing was the idea of diverting cars around a bus in the middle of a road. But it was too late for me to pull a Sabrina act. I'd already committed myself.

For safety reasons, Tom told us he didn't want people straggling along the road, so that the pair who was replaced must immediately return to the bus. "It'll be just like the changing of the guard at Buckingham Palace," he quipped, which amused everyone.

When it came time for my tour of duty with Daisy, the whole operation was running like clockwork. Tom told us when to get off the bus and we headed toward Priscilla and Peter, who were standing over the crest of the hill. They seemed so deeply involved in whatever they were talking about that I wasn't sure they knew the purpose of their being there. We were practically on top of them when they noticed us. I was tempted to make some cutting remark about them shirking their duty, but Daisy did it for me.

"I don't think you two would see a car until it hit you," she kidded.

"You're right," Priscilla remarked, smiling. She didn't seem at all perturbed by Daisy's teasing.

Peter laughed. "Fortunately, there aren't too many cars that come along here. We figured we could afford to live dangerously."

"I guess they're replacing us," Priscilla said, turning to Peter. "We better get out of their way."

"You're right, Pris. We don't want to be responsible for gumming up Tom's operation."

Then, quite unobtrusively, but I couldn't help noticing, he put his hand on Priscilla's elbow and the two of them ambled off, chatting together amiably, oblivious to anything else.

I was unreasonably bothered by the idea that Peter was even remotely interested in Priscilla. Why should I care? I liked Priscilla, too, but she certainly didn't seem his type.

Daisy, the mindreader, remarked, "They're an unlikely couple."

"Sure are."

"Both nice, but such different personalities."

Before she continued analyzing their relationship, a car came barreling up the road. We held up our hands, indicating there was trouble ahead, and it immediately slowed down.

A jovial-looking man with a flushed face and a heavy cockney accent stuck his head out the window. "Never seen such pretty bobbies in my life. What's going on?"

"Our bus was forced off the road by some crazy driver, so be careful going around the bend," Daisy advised.

"Has anyone gone for help?"

"Yes, thanks," I said. "We should be getting towed away very soon."

"I hope so, because you lovely ladies are going to get soaked," he said, as he picked up speed and threw us a kiss goodbye.

His car wasn't even out of sight when his prediction came true and it started to drizzle. "Just our luck," Daisy groaned.

"If only that truck would get here! We'll shrivel up if we have to stand here fifteen minutes," I complained.

"Or longer. Probably, our replacements will chicken out, and we'll be stranded."

With that, there was a clap of thunder and what had started as an insignificant shower turned into a steady downpour. The whole situation was so bizarre that Daisy and I cracked up, and the harder it rained, the more we laughed. In seconds we were drenched—hair dripping, clothes clinging to us like paste, sneakers squishing with water. Blinking against the intensity of the rain, we glimpsed the tow truck heading toward us and cheered wildly. Joe and Clyde were crowded in the front cab seat, and taking in our predicament, grinned sympathetically.

"There's no room here," Clyde yelled out the window, "but we'll get things straightened out right away, I hope." The truck moved off and he waved to us as we started sloshing up the hill.

By the time we arrived, the chains from the truck had been attached to the bus and were dragging it out to the road. The pounding rain had miraculously turned into a heavy mist, as though the weather gods were protecting the other members of the choir who had to stand around while the bus was pulled. No one had been inundated like Daisy and me—the other pair had bolted for the protection of the bus once the skies opened—and we were the recipient of some needlessly graphic descriptions that amused us, too. "They look like survivors of the *Titanic!*" "I'd always heard about drowned rats, but now I've seen some."

Mr. Saxe, however, didn't think our condition was so funny, and insisted that we dig out our suitcases as soon as we got to the next village and change our things at the local gas station. We didn't give him an argument, because our moment of martyrdom had passed and we didn't relish the idea of sitting in soggy clothes. But even on the brief ride to the gas station, I was beginning to feel the effects of our sacrificial act evidenced by an uncontrollable fit of shivering. Daisy and I were sitting together since no one else wanted to get near our water-logged bodies. She was aware that I was chilled to the bone and assured me that as soon as I put on something dry, I would be fine.

I did feel less like a wet dishrag when I changed, and towel-dried my hair, but in spite of the warm weather, I felt peculiarly cold. We were running so late that it was decided we should stay in the village for lunch. Tom made arrangements for us to be served at the one modern-looking building around. The restaurant obviously catered to tourists, the food was served cafeteria-style, and a feeble attempt was made to imitate American fare. Bangers and wimpies, an English version of hot dogs and hamburgers, were featured.

Everyone in the choir, as usual, was ready to pig out, but I wasn't the least bit hungry and settled for a cup of tea. I was one of the last in line and there were only a couple of empty places. One of them was at a table where Peter and Priscilla were sitting. I certainly didn't want to intrude on them, so I sat down at a table for six. The only vacant chair happened to face them, and I had to make a point of not staring in their direction.

I tried to appear a lot more animated than I felt and made a special effort to participate in the conversation. I've never liked telling people I didn't feel well since it always seemed like admitting defeat. If I was unusually quiet and not eating, I might invite some questions regarding my health. So I babbled on, with the rest of them, about Joe's heroic driving, how he'd saved the world's greatest high school choir from disaster, how I couldn't believe we were on the last week of the tour. Also, strangely enough, I didn't want Peter to think I wasn't enjoying myself.

Tom had been sitting at a table with Mr. Saxe, Julie, and Clyde, and I didn't think he noticed me. But when I got up to get a second cup of tea, he immediately got up from where he was sitting and followed me.

"I trust you're feeling fit again," he said, blocking my way as I started to get in the cafeteria line.

"I'm fine," I assured him.

"That's great, because we've just been discussing our schedule, and we're going to have a free afternoon and evening tomorrow. I've got great plans for us."

"For us?" I repeated, and his deep blue eyes had their usual magnetic effect on me.

"I'm going to show you Cambridge," he whispered.

"Cambridge," I gasped.

"Sshhh," he said, putting his hand softly across my mouth. "I don't want to advertise it." Then, in a normal voice, "Better get in line now."

I automatically did what he said. My knees had turned to Jell-O and my stomach was doing flip-flops, which had nothing to do with the state of my health.

I was in a daze as I carried my tea back to my table, but I also was aware, for the first time that day, of Peter looking at me. He was frowning slightly, and unless my imagination was running wild, he was also, almost imperceptibly, shaking his head.

10

There was a general letdown the remainder of the ride, but our spirits revived considerably when we saw our hotel in London. Probably because it was the end of the trip, and our last stop, EIE had arranged for us to stay in relative elegance. Daisy and I had a double room, and it was considerably larger than any of the others we had occupied. But the biggest luxury of all was a connecting bathroom, and the fact that we shared it with Sabrina and Helene didn't lessen my enthusiasm. Anything was better than walking a mile down the hall or going outside just to take a shower.

Daisy and I quickly unpacked our things and then went downstairs to investigate the rest of the hotel aptly named Paragon. It retained all the elements of a bygone age, including a banquet hall, a gaming room, where one could imagine frock-coated gents playing whist and snooker, a music room, and even the old-world charm of a plant room.

Because of our delay, Tom had announced that we would forego the usual rehearsal and settle for a warm-up at the school where the concert was to take place. We didn't have much time, so Daisy and I raced around the hotel like a couple of cartoon characters, then rushed back to our room to change into our concert clothes, and back downstairs onto the bus.

The concert, scheduled for seven o'clock, was programmed for an hour of music. Then there was to be a brief reception. It was the first time I was almost too tired to enjoy singing, and I couldn't wait until the evening was over. On the ride back to the Paragon, Mr. Saxe implied that the day's adventure had taken its toll.

"You've all come through for me, but please take it easy tonight and go to bed early. I don't want us to get a reputation as the Haggard High School singers."

There were some scattered mumblings and groans. "We've only got a few nights left, Mr. Saxe," Kiki complained.

"I know, Kiki, but if you're exhausted you won't enjoy any of them. And remember, we want our final concert, which is only three days off, to be a blockbuster."

"But tomorrow's a free day, which means we can sleep late," Kiki argued.

"If you sleep late, you'll kill half the day," he countered.

"Oh yeah," she conceded, as though some complicated mathematical calculation had been made clear to her.

I, personally, couldn't wait to go to sleep. Not only did I feel like a hundred years old, but no matter how hard I tried to ignore it, my throat felt scratchy. I was sure a good night's sleep after a hot bath would cure me.

As I got off the bus, Tom surreptitiously slipped me a note. The minute I got upstairs, I ducked into the bathroom, locked both doors, and started running the water in the tub. Then I sat on the edge of the tub and carefully unfolded the paper that I had been clutching.

> Beth, love, meet me in
> the plant room tomorrow at
> noon, and we'll set off for
> Cambridge. Be discreet, dearest.
>   T.

I had the note memorized by the time I had taken off my clothes and eased myself into the tub. The faint annoyance I felt when I saw that every available space in the bathroom had been taken over by Helene and Sabrina promptly disappeared. What difference did it make if their makeup, body lotions, shampoo, hair dryers, cotton balls, nail files, and even their laundry was strung out all over the place? That wasn't the least bit important compared to the fact that Tom had singled me out to take to Cambridge.

Beth, love . . . dearest, he had written. I closed my eyes and luxuriated in the warmth of the water and the delicious anticipation of the next day. I was lulled into a semiconscious state, and might have actually fallen sound asleep if a sharp voice hadn't startled me.

"Are you planning on staying in there all night?" It was Sabrina, sounding very impatient.

"Oh no," I replied, not quite sure how long I'd been soaking. "I'm getting out right away."

I hurriedly stood up, splashing water on the floor in the process, blotted myself dry, mopped up the floor with my towel, picked up my clothes, grabbed Tom's scrap of paper, which had taken on the proportions of an epic love poem, unlocked both doors, and fell into bed without bothering to put on my nightshirt. I still had the presence of mind to stick the note under my pillow, more comforting than any teddy bear.

Daisy was already in bed and mumbled something about being too tired to even brush her teeth. "Night," she said, and immediately she conked out.

When I awoke the next morning, there was no sign of Daisy. To my horror, I thought I might have been too late to meet Tom, and frantically groped for my watch. My eyes were blurry, but with enormous relief I could see it was only a little after eleven, which gave me plenty of time to get ready.

Daisy had made her bed and left a note on the pillow. I leaped out of bed, but sank back down immediately because I was overcome with a wave of dizziness. It passed quickly, but I forced myself to move more slowly and reached for her note.

> You were sleeping so soundly, I didn't have the heart to wake you. A bunch of us are going to check out the original Laura Ashley. We'll be there all morning if you want to catch up with us.

I was glad that I didn't have to tell Daisy I was off to Cambridge with Tom. Since she had already left, I could be discreet without being deceptive.

I went into the bathroom and as I closed the door to Helene and Sabrina's room, I saw that it was deserted. Apparently I was the last one to get up.

I glanced in the mirror over the sink as I started to brush my teeth, and my eyes were puffy. After rinsing out my mouth, I splashed cold water on my face, which helped a little. My throat was dry and since I didn't have salt or mouthwash, I gargled with hot water from the tap. With my slight dizziness, slitty eyes, and incipient sore throat, I was a mess.

I wasn't really sick—I was sure my temperature was normal—so I pretended to myself that I was only suffering the aftermath of yesterday's exposure and fatigue. Nothing serious. A trip to Cambridge wouldn't be that strenuous; Tom would do all the driving; I would sit back and relax; and the whole excursion would make me feel a lot better than holing up alone in the hotel.

I carefully selected what I would wear: a long-sleeved Gibson-girl blouse, dark-blue skirt patterned with tiny yellow and white flowers, and sandals. I put everything on Daisy's bed and then stretched out on mine, wanting to preserve every last bit of strength. A few more minutes of relaxing was all I needed to win a 4-H contest. I'll be fine, I'll be fine, I'll be fine, kept echoing in my mind, but the idea of being with Tom all afternoon and evening was hardly conducive to rest and I decided to get ready.

I haphazardly made the bed—didn't want to waste energy on that—and then in slow motion got dressed and applied a little blush-on and lip gloss. A final inspection in the mirror convinced me that I no longer had that waiflike wan look, and even my eyes looked less piggy.

There was still time for a cup of tea, so I took the lift down to the lobby and headed directly for the dining room. A few tables were occupied, but there wasn't a sign of anyone from the choir. More proof of Tom's cleverness! By planning for us to meet at noon, he knew that everyone in our group would be doing his or her own thing, and we could avoid curious looks and comments.

The sun poured through the casement windows of the old-fashioned dining room, and a waitress in a freshly starched uniform took my order for a pot of tea. I still had twelve minutes to kill, and sipped it slowly, pacing myself so that I wouldn't be hanging around the plant room, waiting for Tom and feeling like an abandoned sapling.

The tea tasted delicious, but there was no denying that every time I swallowed, my throat felt funny, although not nearly sore enough to make me break my date with Tom. I'd have to be a hospital case for that to happen! However, I did have a definite pang of guilt when I recalled Mr. Saxe cautioning us about health. Periodically, especially during the early days of our rehearsing back in the States, he had impressed on us the necessity of getting enough rest, protecting ourselves from colds, taking special care if we had the vaguest tickling in our throats.

"I don't want to turn you into a bunch of hypochondriacs," he said, "but singing with a sore throat is like playing football with a pulled tendon. Not only does your performance suffer, but you make it tough on the rest of the team. And if you're really not feeling well, it's up to you to volunteer *not* to sing."

Well, I told myself, I wasn't at that stage yet, I had all the rest of the day and night to get better, and the bottom line was that I was willing to risk a lot more than a stupid sore throat if it meant being with Tom.

I paid my bill and although my heart was racing, I strolled in the most leisurely way possible towards the plant room. I didn't want to appear overly eager or rushed for two reasons. First, if there were some stray choristers around, I didn't want to draw attention to myself. Second, when Tom saw me, I wanted to seem cool and sophisticated, as if it wasn't a bit unusual for a Cambridge man to want to show me his university.

Tom was already there, inspecting a ficus tree, when I entered the plant room.

"Lovely, isn't it?" I remarked.

He looked at me, appraisingly, and flashed me that brilliant, unnerving smile. "Smashing," he said, and I knew he wasn't referring to the ficus.

Tom was wearing a pale-blue crewneck sweater over a beige-colored shirt with a paisley ascot tucked casually around his neck, and well-creased khaki slacks. For a second I couldn't think of anything to say, and I couldn't take my eyes off him. "Smashing," I muttered, finally, allowing him to interpret that remark any way he pleased.

He chuckled knowingly, and said, "We better get started." He took me by the hand and walked briskly down the hall through the lobby and onto the street. It was a gorgeous sunny day with a slight breeze coming from the north. A perfect day for a drive, I thought, until Tom stopped in front of an open two-seated MG convertible.

"Yours?" I asked, inanely.

"I'm not really the criminal type, even though I break the courier rules."

"I wasn't expecting you to have an open car."

"You're not worried about your hair getting mussed, I hope."

"Of course not."

"There's an extra scarf in the glove compartment for just that purpose."

"Standard equipment for convertibles?"

He laughed, guided me around to the passenger side, and held the door open as I climbed into the bucket seat. I was glad I'd remembered at the last minute to bring a cardigan, which I'd stuffed into my hobo bag, along with a bunch of tissues. I dug out the sweater and then shoved the bag behind the seat, where I saw Tom's raincoat and umbrella. I must have frowned, thinking about the possibility of rain, and Tom said, "Why so worried?"

"Surprised you brought a raincoat, that's all."

"You never know in this part of the world what might happen."

"Maybe I should go back and get mine."

"Don't worry, darling, I'll take care of you." He slammed the door on my side, and went around to the driver's seat while I smiled to myself. Breaking courier rules and a possible case of pneumonia seemed a small price to pay for what was sure to be my day of days.

Tom skillfully maneuvered the MG through the congested London traffic and briefed me on what to expect. He warned me that the university would seem relatively deserted during the "vac" term, which I figured out meant vacation.

"There'll still be some med and law students around, but not nearly the quantity we have during the regular term."

"Is there a difference between Cambridge and Oxford?"

"Enormous," he answered, laughing. I had a feeling he was making fun of me.

"Well, how am I supposed to know?" I asked defensively.

"You don't really expect an unbiased answer from me, do you?" He turned his head to face me, half smiling, and I wondered why I got so uptight around Tom, even when he hadn't said anything personal.

"I've heard them referred to as Oxbridge," I said, trying to show I wasn't totally ignorant.

"Don't ever breathe a word of this," he said, "but they have been called the sister universities."

Then we both laughed, and I momentarily relaxed, thinking I *was* capable of carrying on a reasonable conversation with Tom. I leaned back, enjoying being in an open car, until we got out of the city and onto the highway. Then Tom, whether to make up for lost time or to prove his macho, proceeded to burn up the road. I buttoned my sweater and instinctively slunk down in the seat, hoping to protect myself from the relentless breeze.

"You're not frightened, are you?" Tom asked solicitously.

"No," I replied indignantly. The last impression I wanted to make was of being a coward.

"You don't like open roadsters?"

"Sure I do." I would rather have died than admit that I wanted him to put up the top, although dying seemed like a distinct possibility if he went any faster. However, I forced myself to sit up straight and braced myself against the wind, determined to appear less like a wimp.

Tom did most of the talking, filling me in on the history of Cambridge University which began in the thirteenth century, consists of twenty-three colleges, the oldest being Peterhouse, which originated in 1284, and the newest, Robinson, a coed college opened by the Queen in 1977, and the reason for the name, Cambridge. Even I could guess that the town was on the site of a bridge on the river Cam!

I tried to show my interest by interjecting with comments of my own. "That's fascinating!" "Oh, really?" "I didn't know that." Also, if I concentrated on listening, I wouldn't worry about the fact that my eyes were tearing in spite of my sunglasses, my hair was blowing uncomfortably into my face, nothing like the windswept look one sees in the ads, and that I had to keep clearing my throat in order to repress a cough.

When we arrived in Cambridge, the whole trip was less than two hours, Tom parked the car on a quiet tree-lined street. He got out and as he made his way gracefully to my side of the car to open the door, I saw he was as perfectly groomed as when we started, except for a lock of hair that had fallen over his forehead and made him even more appealing, if that were possible. He held the door for me while I frantically began to make repairs, first struggling to comb through my hair that seemed permanently tangled.

"There's a nice restaurant, the Copper Kettle on Trumpington Street, where we can have lunch and you can freshen up. We're not going to a ball, you know." I couldn't read his expression because he was wearing aviator glasses, but I sensed his impatience and hurried out of the car. Perhaps I'd been imagining his irritation, because he rambled on about the beauties of Cambridge nonstop until we arrived at the restaurant, were seated at a table and ordered our lunch.

I hurried into the ladies' room, allowed myself the luxury of a coughing fit, washed my tear-streaked face, vigorously brushed my hair, and dusted my cheeks with blush-on. There was nothing I could do about the hollow look around my eyes, but at least I looked presentable.

As I headed back for the table, I saw Tom holding a stein of beer, and chatting up a girl whose back was to me. He looked very animated, and involved, but when

I approached he immediately stood up, pulled back my chair, and introduced us. "Beth, this is Daphne, a classmate who's here for the summer term." Then, he added unnecessarily, "The only good reason for going to summer school."

Daphne had dark voluptuous looks and was wearing a low-cut peasant blouse that didn't exactly hide her figure. "Hello, Beth. You'll excuse me if I have to run. My friends are waiting." She seemed remarkably poised, and I felt much younger than my sixteen years.

I noticed Tom followed her with his eyes until she was out of sight. Was it my imagination again, or did he reluctantly turn his attention to me?

The sandwiches we ordered were served and as we munched on them, Tom focused on me so completely that I stopped worrying about other women in his life.

"What do you want to do with your life professionally?" he began. "With a voice like yours, it must have something to do with singing."

"That's right," I answered, "but I'm not sure what yet."

"You've not only got the voice, but the looks. You could be on the stage, in the movies. There are endless possibilities."

"You really think so?"

"Absolutely! Especially if you studied acting."

"I never thought of that."

"There are so few good singers who can act. If you mastered that, you could write your own ticket. Musicals, operas, anything."

I'd only been drinking a cola, but I suddenly felt very heady, seeing myself as Eliza Doolittle in *My Fair Lady,* Maria in *West Side Story,* or perhaps Violetta in *La Traviata.* As if to feed my fantasy, Tom said, "I know you'll always be performing to a full house, but promise to reserve one on the aisle for me."

"Of course!" I said, and then blushed with embarrassment because I'd been so carried away.

"Want some dessert?" he asked, tactfully helping me to reenter the real world.

"No thanks," I muttered.

"Then we better get started. If we return to London at a reasonable hour, there won't be any raised eyebrows."

"I hope you don't get in trouble because of me."

"Don't worry, love. It's too near the end of the tour to fire me, and this is the last summer I plan to work for EIE, anyway."

"You don't like being a courier?"

"I didn't say that."

He didn't seem to want to continue the discussion, and besides, the waitress had come with the check. But I couldn't resist asking him about his professional plans.

"Today is your day, Beth. We'll talk about me next time."

I thought that was a curious response but I let it pass. It made me feel good to know there would be a next time, and I couldn't remember anyone ever saying "today is your day."

When we got outside, Tom put his arm through mine and announced that he would show me the "quintessential" Cambridge, beginning at the top of Bridge Street. For the next few hours we ambled through the extraordinarily peaceful quadrangles of the colleges. The cobblestone courtyard of Trinity was my favorite. Tom told me it was Sir Isaac Newton's college and pointed out an apple tree that was supposedly the descendant of the one that caused Newton to formulate the laws of gravity. Next, we browsed briefly in a humungus bookshop on Trinity Street. I'd never seen such an incredible number of sections, with subjects ranging from hymenopterous insects to epistemology.

Cambridge was turning out to be everything I imagined it would be, but my first view of the Cam and the "Backs," the extensive parkland that extends along the river behind several colleges, was overwhelming. There were couples punting on the Cam and I could barely contain my excitement when Tom suggested we hire a punt from Trinity. What could be more romantic!

I bruised my knee climbing into the boat, which made me feel less like a nineteenth-century femme fatale than a modern spaz. But once I settled onto a seat, we shoved off, and Tom guided the boat along the river with the expertise of a gondolier, I was "transported" in every sense of the word. As we drifted along, I soaked in the sights—architecture ranging from Gothic and Tudor to modern, and the carefully landscaped gardens that graced the riverside colleges. I was thinking how contented I would be to spend the rest of the afternoon on the Cam, when Tom suddenly steered the boat around and headed for our starting point.

"We're not going back already!" I exclaimed.

"I'm enjoying this, too, but part of your Cambridge education is to attend Evensong at King's College. I promise you, you won't regret it."

"But do we have to go so early?" I persisted.

"Look, Beth," he snapped, "Evensong begins at five-thirty, and it's already quarter to. Or do you want to take over, now?"

"Course not," I replied, shocked at his sudden outburst.

He had been punting perfectly, smoothly dipping the long pole into the river bottom and propelling us forward at a steady speed. But he momentarily lost control and slapped the water with the pole, splashing me in the process. I couldn't help laughing, but Tom looked grim as he struggled to regain his balance and get the boat back on course.

"That was fun," I said lightly, once I saw we had avoided any serious mishap, but Tom obviously didn't see it that way. He remained silent until we were safely returned to the rental place and had disembarked.

I was wondering if maybe it had been my fault, that somehow I'd upset his rhythm, and that he'd stay mad at me forever, when he turned to me with his most engaging smile. "Forgive me, darling, I'm just so anxious for you to see everything, and if we don't keep to our time schedule it won't happen—especially if we take time out for an unplanned dousing in the river."

"Did you really think we might capsize?" I thought perhaps I had been a bit too cavalier about that possibility.

"It's been known to happen, but I saved you from that and now we must press on."

He walked briskly, and his stride was so much longer than mine that I had trouble keeping up with him. However, I wasn't about to hang back and risk getting him upset again. I hadn't thought about my health since we'd arrived in Cambridge, probably because there were so many other distractions, but as I struggled to match his pace, my breathing became heavier and heavier. In fact, I was the living example of a game that Daisy, Patsy, and I used to play called "Sick," in the days when we didn't talk so much about boys. The point of the game was to see who could come up with the most original ailments, and at the moment I felt I had all of them! My teeth were wearing fur jackets, my hair hurt, my skin was inside out, and there were canoes in my calves.

I was literally gasping for breath when we arrived at King's College, but as soon as we settled down in the majestic chapel, I forgot all about my symptoms. The combination of perfectly attuned organ and choir music, the prism of light coming through the exquisite stained glass windows and reflected on the stone floor of the chapel, and the view of the Rubens painting, *The Adoration of the Magi*, under the east window was enough to make me forgive Tom for any discomfort he had caused me. He was Mr. Wonderful, I thought, and if he ever got peevish, it was my fault.

It was twilight when the service was over, and I felt a bittersweet pang of regret when I realized my day of days was drawing to a close. I was so moved by Evensong that I didn't want to say anything; it was really beyond words. We fell into the crowd pouring out of the chapel, and it came as a shock that Tom didn't share my serene mood. Before we even got outside, he stated in a harsh voice, "There's one more thing you must see before we return to London, and that's the view from Clare bridge."

I thought perhaps I was being oversensitive and Tom wasn't being severe at all. After all, he'd been to King's Chapel many times and there was no reason for him to be totally in sync with how I was feeling.

"I'd love to see it," I said, and this time I put my arm through his. I wanted him to know how much I'd enjoyed everything, since it was possible that he'd interpreted my silence as indifference. But I still couldn't think of the right thing to say.

Again, he moved so fast I got the impression he was anxious to wind up our date, but still show me everything so that I couldn't accuse him of not providing me with the crème de la crème treatment.

"Not so fast," I pleaded. "The bridge isn't going to disappear."

"Sorry, love, I'm just anxious for you to see the gardens from the bridge in an impressionistic light. It's the kind of painterly sight that would have inspired van Gogh or Manet. If we dawdle, you'll miss what I'm talking about."

I believed him implicitly, and mentally kicked myself for being so suspicious. Why on earth would he have bothered to spend so much time with me if he didn't care? He had made such an effort to entertain and educate me, I felt indebted to him. And he knew so much! I wasn't even sure what "painterly" meant, and he'd just tossed it off like he'd said the sky was blue.

He was right about Clare bridge, too, where we could see the spacious gardens of the colleges, more beautiful than ever in the late afternoon light. I never thought of a bridge being romantic, but that's exactly what it was.

"Well, Beth, this is the last stop," Tom proclaimed. "Did Cambridge live up to your expectations?"

"Oh, yes," I breathed, and without thinking tilted my head toward him, inviting a kiss.

He took the hint and pressed his lips against mine, but then quickly backed away. I was all set to be hurt, but he immediately explained: "Bad form to have any public display of emotion."

"Of course," I said, embarrassed at my impulsive behavior, although I'd only seen one or two couples passing by, and at the moment we were alone.

"We've got to get started. Never know what traffic will be like."

"I know," I agreed, robotlike, and let him lead me by the hand towards the car.

"Gorgeous night," he remarked, once we'd settled into the bucket seats. "Trust you're still game for riding with the top down."

"Sure," I lied. "But I think I might borrow that scarf."

Tom reached in the glove compartment and handed me a large silk kerchief which I tied around my head, faintly conscious of its perfumed fragrance. How many others had worn this scarf? I really didn't want to know, Tom probably wouldn't tell me, and I had to guard against bad form.

We hardly spoke at all while Tom concentrated on driving and I thought all about what had transpired, my feelings about Tom, my gnawing doubt that we weren't really sharing what I'd read about as a companionable silence.

"Before we hit the highway, do you want to get something to eat?" Tom could never be accused of not doing the correct thing.

"I'm not the least bit hungry, but what about you?"

"I'm not, either. Seems we just finished lunch."

Then, as if to indicate that he was definitely not in the mood for conversation, he put on the radio. Some news commentator droned on about the prime minister's plan to control inflation, and I found myself nodding off, until we hit the highway. Tom accelerated the engine, and with the cold night air and the velocity of the wind, I felt we had entered the Arctic zone.

"It's freezing," I cried out, and actually could hear my teeth beginning to chatter.

"Don't tell me you want the top up now?"

"I'm sorry, Tom, but I didn't realize it would be this cold."

"I'll have to get off the highway; I can't stop here."

"It's okay," I said, gritting my teeth. "I'll get used to it."

"Good girl," he approved, "No point in having an open car if we keep it closed."

"Right," I mumbled, and scrunched down, my arms crossed in front of me as though that would help protect me from the elements.

Tom did make fantastic time, but by the time he pulled up to the hotel I was congealed with cold. "Want a nightcap, love?" he asked, before getting out of the car.

"No thanks, I'm just interested in thawing out."

"You Yankees aren't so rugged as you pretend." He leaned across and opened the door on my side, brushing his lips against my cheek in the process.

"You're not getting out?" I asked.

"I have to fill up with petrol, and you look like you're ready to sack out."

"I am," I admitted, "but I hate this to end."

"There'll be other days, darling."

"I hope so. It was wonderful and thanks for everything, Tom."

"My pleasure." He beamed that heartbreak smile at me and at the same time revved up the motor. I couldn't help feeling I was being dismissed, but he did wait while I got out, closed the door, and trudged into the lobby. I turned around to wave goodbye, and he blew me a kiss.

Perfect timing again, I thought, going into the elevator. It was a little past nine—too late for anyone to still be having dinner in the dining room, and too early for them not to be out on the town. No one was around, so

I had the bathroom to myself, but I was too tired to take a bath. I washed quickly, put a sweater on over my nightshirt, and popped two aspirin into my mouth. My shivers gradually subsided as I buried myself under the blankets, but there was no denying it: my throat was killing me.

11

I slept fitfully, the night demons vying for attention, and I didn t know which one should have priority. I worried about the impression I'd made on Tom, about my throat constricting, about Daisy's reaction to my vanishing act. In the wee hours of the night, I thought I'd been an airhead not to leave her a note swearing her to secrecy but telling her where I'd gone. I was almost tempted to wake her up and explain how everything had happened so fast I hadn't had time, but I decided to wait until morning.

Finally, emotionally and physically wiped out, I fell into a druglike sleep. Daisy was already getting dressed when I awakened. I had trouble finding my voice, but I wanted to be relieved of my burden of guilt and said hoarsely, even before saying "good morning," "I was in Cambridge yesterday with Tom."

"So I heard."

I couldn't believe my ears. Who could have told her? "How did you find out? No one was supposed to know."

"Sabrina let the cat out of the bag."

"Sabrina?"

"We were all hanging around Laura Ashley's, and Patsy said something about whether you'd show up or not."

"And?"

"And Sabrina let it be known that you had gone off to Cambridge with Tom for the day."

"How did she know?"

"If you didn't tell her, I guess he did."

"I can't believe that. He made me promise to be discreet." I was in a state of shock, but managed to ask, "What else did Sabrina say?"

"Something about you not being back till nine o'clock."

"But why would he have told her?"

"Who knows? Maybe she asked him to spend the day with her, and he had to explain that you'd gotten to him first."

"You know I'd never do that, no matter how liberated." I laughed weakly, but Daisy knew me too well not to recognize that I was really undone.

"Well, you arrived here in one piece, although your voice sounds a little weird. Are you feeling okay?"

"Just a little head cold."

"We have a rehearsal in thirty minutes, and you better get rolling. Our big concert is tomorrow, and we don't want Saxe to have a nervous breakdown because you're late."

"I'll be there on time."

"You want me to wait for you?"

"No thanks, I'll move faster if I'm alone."

As soon as Daisy left, I dragged myself into the bathroom where I washed and brushed and gargled. My throat felt like a bulldozer was working on it, but I was sure some hot tea would help. I got dressed as quickly as possible and went to the dining room.

Daisy was sitting alone at a table. As I headed for it, I passed Tom, sitting with a bunch of kids. He looked up, gave me a quick wink as though nothing was unusual, and then ignored me. He didn't look a bit guilty, but perhaps that was because he wasn't aware that I knew he had confided in Sabrina about *us*. My brain was a little fuzzy and I decided to worry about that later. At that moment, I had to think about getting my voice workable.

It was hard to swallow the tea I'd ordered, and Daisy frowned as she saw me making faces just trying to get it down.

"Maybe you should skip this morning's rehearsal," she suggested.

"No way! I'll take it easy this afternoon and I'll be fine. I know how to sing above a cold, you know."

"If you say so, but the final concert is the most important, and you wouldn't want to miss that."

"I'm not about to miss any of them."

"Don't you think you should alert Saxe, at least?"

"Daisy, I'm going to sing and that's final!" I knew Daisy had my best interests at heart, but I refused to face the idea of *not* singing.

However, I guess it was naive of me to think Saxe wouldn't pick up immediately on the fact that I wasn't up to par. Even before I rehearsed my solo, he zeroed in on the fact that I was straining. As soon as we had our first break, he called me aside.

"What's wrong, Beth? You sound shaky."

"I've got a little cold, that's all."

"Do you think you can sing at the concert tonight?"

"Of course, I can. I know how to use my head tones when I have a cold."

"I don't want you pushing yourself if you're not well."

"I'm fine," I insisted, and added meekly, "except for this cold."

He looked at me skeptically and said, "If you say so. But in order to preserve your vocal chords, I won't have you work on your solo now. I'll alert Peter, and you can warm up with him later this afternoon."

"Oh, thanks, Mr. Saxe. I promise I'll rest all day, and I'll be ready for the performance."

"If you're not, let me know. I'm going to let Greta rehearse your solo this morning, just in case."

"Okay," I sighed, knowing that was a precautionary measure I couldn't stop. "But I'll be up for it tonight, honest!"

Mr. Saxe meticulously coached Greta through my aria, until he got the exact sound he wanted. She had a pure white tone, not really as strong as mine, but I knew she could pull off an excellent performance. However, much as I liked Greta and appreciated her support of me, I didn't want anyone to take over my role. Since there were a number of times in other rehearsals when Saxe had asked her to sing solo, no one made any comment. But I was conscious that this time he wanted her to be perfectly prepared, and there was no denying that I felt threatened.

When the rehearsal was over, I whispered to Daisy that I was going to devote the rest of the day to improving my health. No point in advertising the fact that I was under the weather. Then I went over to the piano and spoke to Peter, who was gathering his music together. I felt a little funny asking him for a favor, since we'd hardly said two words to each other for the past twenty-four hours, so I got right to the point.

"Will you meet me here later this afternoon so I can warm up for tonight? Mr. Saxe said I . . ."

"I know," he said evenly. "Is five o'clock okay?"

"Five is fine," I answered.

"See ya later," he said, "I've got to run now."

"See ya," I said, watching him rush off, and wondering if he was meeting Priscilla and telling myself it didn't matter. I had other things to think about, mainly getting well.

I wended my way to the pharmacy down the block and bought an array of medicines—antiseptic mouth wash, lozenges, cough drops, vapor rub, and a jar of honey, known for its soothing qualities. On my way back to my room, I stopped in the dining room and arranged for a pot of hot water and tea bags to be sent to my room. The rest of the afternoon, I played hospital, first rubbing that loathsome vapor rub on my chest, then gulping down teaspoonfuls of tea and honey, sucking on cough drops, gargling, and then repeating the whole procedure. I dozed on and off, hoping my crash program would result in a miracle cure, but by the time I was supposed to meet Peter in the music room, I still felt crummy. In addition, I was woozy because I'd skipped lunch—the idea of food repelled me—and cough drops did not provide much nourishment. However, I was determined not to give in.

Peter was already playing some jazz when I arrived in the music room. I stood in the doorway listening, awed at his versatility. After a few moments, he noticed me and abruptly stopped playing.

"Keep going," I urged. "It sounds great." My voice sounded strange to me, but I hoped no one else would notice.

"Are you here to practice the soprano solo or the bass?" he asked.

"That bad?" I said, moving toward the piano.

"You don't sound like you, but then I'm not sure who you really are, anyway."

I hadn't planned to get into a personal discussion, but to my surprise I found myself saying, "You're not mad at me, are you?"

Peter looked down at the keyboard, and idly played a few chords.

"Why should I be?"

"Don't know. Just thought you've been avoiding me lately." What I really meant was that he'd been spending all his time with Priscilla.

Then, totally out of character, he banged a loud chord on the piano and shouted, "I haven't been avoiding you. You're so bewitched by that phony English charm that you can't see straight. You don't know when you've been taken for a ride, and I don't mean in an open convertible."

"What do you mean, taken for a ride! And how do you know about the open convertible?"

"Everybody knows, except maybe Mr. Saxe."

"Everybody," I murmured, unable to grasp what Peter was telling me.

"Look, Beth, it's none of my business, and besides, we're here for a purpose. Let's get started on the Bach."

"Let's," I agreed, afraid to hear any more critical comments about Tom.

I was trembling slightly, a reaction to Peter's outburst as well as my physical weakness, but I poised myself beside the piano, knowing I had to get through this practice session. My voice sounded strained from the beginning—I could barely reach the high notes—and it became thinner and thinner. However, I managed to finish the aria without breaking down. In the past, Peter would make some comment, invariably complimentary, whenever I warmed up with him, but this time he messed around with the sheet music and said nothing.

"Well?" I said finally, breaking the ominous silence.

His brow wrinkled, and his eyes which had flashed with anger earlier, looked genuinely worried.

"The truth is, Beth, I don't think you should sing tonight."

"That's ridiculous! I got through the aria, didn't I?"

"Barely. At the end, you were hanging on by a thin reed."

"But I did get through it and I'm not giving up now because of a stupid sniffle."

"Why not save yourself for the final concert? Jeremy Rivers will be in the audience for that one, and you'll probably be okay by then."

"I'm okay now."

"You're not, Beth. Face it. It's not the end of the world if an understudy takes over. It even happens at the Met."

"I'm not giving in to this!"

"You're making a mistake, and not just musically."

"What's that supposed to mean?"

"You can figure it out. What's wrong with giving someone else a chance?"

"You just don't understand."

"Guess not."

"I thought you were my friend," I croaked, wanting to end the conversation, and moving toward the door.

"I am," I heard him say softly as I was leaving. "I am."

Dinner was scheduled for six o'clock so I went directly to the dining room. I knew I had to eat something in order not to pass out, although I still wasn't hungry. It was a few minutes before six and Flos and Mike were the only ones in the dining room. They motioned to me to join them, and I was grateful for the distraction, although I kept thinking about Peter's advice. If anything, my resolve to perform that night was stronger than ever. Peter was a fine musician, but his instrument was the piano, not voice. I knew more about singing, and my capabilities, than he did. Besides, I might feel better after I ate something.

The choir poured into the dining room precisely at six, our table was immediately filled, and the set menu of soup, steak, and chips was served. I didn't want to make a scene, but after finishing my soup and picking at the main course, as unobtrusively as possible, I slipped away. It wasn't just my disinterest in food, but I actually experienced a moment of panic about the concert. If I continued my treatment, I'd be okay.

I went upstairs to my room and feverishly gargled until I heard the others coming. Then I fortified myself with two aspirins, shoved the medicines in the cabinet over the sink, no one else bothered to use the cabinet, and flew into our room where as casually as possible I began changing into my choir clothes.

"How are you feeling?" Daisy asked, as soon as she came into our room.

"Fine, I think." I wasn't sure myself how sick I was at that point, but my chest definitely felt congested and I knew I was suffering from more than your everyday ordinary sniffle. But still, I could make it if I'd hung in this far.

The church was a large modern structure. Tom explained on the way over that it had been reconstructed after being bombed during the war. It had a big, barny quality that had much less appeal than the medieval churches we had sung in throughout England. Was its coldness an omen of how I would be received, or just a reflection of my mood? This was not a time for me to get superstitious and philosophical. I had to concentrate on getting my act together!

We assembled in the waiting room, and Mr. Saxe cornered me. I was hoping to avoid any questions, but that was absurd. Of course he wanted to know how I was feeling.

"Are you able to sing, Beth?"

I nodded my head yes, not trusting myself to speak in a normal voice. If my speaking voice betrayed me, he'd never let me go on.

"You're sure?" His eyes were so penetrating that I had to look down.

"Uh huh," I replied, fervently hoping that the inquisition would end.

Then, to my enormous relief, Tom announced that it was time for us to line up. "You're on in two minutes. And I think you should know, choir, that your reputation has preceded you. There's not an empty seat out there."

There was a lot of tittering at that remark, but I felt a cold shiver run through me. The idea of a full house was usually exciting, but this time I was frightened. As we marched on stage, I tried desperately to relax. If I was tense, my throat would tighten up irreparably, and I couldn't afford to compound my problem.

I was conscious of a zillion things happening at once: The lights dimmed, the audience was a clapping monster, Mr. Saxe was about to impale us with his baton, piano music was being played, and my knees were buckling. The fact that I was able to stand up was a triumph. My throat was constricting uncontrollably and I decided to fake it, just mouthing the words of the madrigals. If I held back singing with the chorus, I'd be ready for my solo.

There was a pause after the first set of madrigals was completed, and while the audience applauded, Mr. Saxe glared at me angrily. He knew I wasn't singing, and *I* knew the soprano section was noticeably weakened. I forced myself to sing the next set in spite of how much it hurt. My warm-up with Peter was a breeze compared to what I was going through.

Then it was time for my solo and I stepped forward. I was totally unstrung; my legs shook, beads of perspiration covered my forehead, and I dug my fingernails so deep into my palms that I wouldn't have been surprised if my hands bled. Through a misty blur, I saw Mr. Saxe cue Peter, then nod to me. *Be brave, be brave,* I told myself, but after the first phrase I knew I was in deep trouble. I couldn't sustain any notes, and my voice began to crack. By the third measure of the second phrase, all that came out was an unpleasant raspy sound and I knew I was finished.

Mr. Saxe dropped his baton and indicated with his head that I should leave the stage. As I slumped off, unable to maintain any semblance of dignity, there were audible gasps from the audience. Next, I heard Mr. Saxe saying, "We're very sorry that we cannot complete the Bach. Our soprano, Miss Farley, has been fighting a cold for the past few days, and unfortunately it seems to have gotten the best of her. We will continue our program with the Bartok songs."

I collapsed on a bench in the waiting room, numb with humiliation. I only wanted to hide—from everyone, including myself—but there was no place to go. I recalled a line from Edith Wharton's *House of Mirth* when the heroine was in the depths of despair: "It was easy enough to despise the world, but decidedly difficult to find any other habitable region." How could I face Mr. Saxe, the chorus, my friends—especially Daisy and Peter, who had both tried to talk me out of singing? Why hadn't I listened to them? I had been self-serving and selfish. Peter had said, "You're making a mistake, and not just musically." Now I understood clearly what he meant. I buried my head in my hands, wishing I could weep, but my tears were dry, the cruelest tears of all.

I escaped from the waiting room as soon as I heard the choir singing the final piece, a hymn called *The New Jerusalem*, and boarded the bus. I curled up over two seats in the rear and closed my eyes. I must have succeeded in getting across the message that I didn't want to talk because when the others climbed on they treated me as though I were in the last stages of leprosy. While conversations bubbled around me, I had these crazy feverish thoughts about what it would be like to take a vow of silence and never speak to anyone again.

I continued to play 'possum when we arrived at the hotel and heard everyone scrambling off the bus. Then someone tapped me on the arm and I slowly opened one eye. It was Mr. Saxe, sitting across the aisle, and as a reflex, my body tensed with fear. He had every right to be enraged, but his hand resting gently on my arm, and the sympathetic look in his eyes was reassuring.

"You learned something tonight, Beth, and I don't have to spell it out for you. No one is hurting as much as you are, but now you have to build from this experience. I want you to know I still have faith in you—as an artist, and as a human being."

"Thank you, Mr. Saxe," I stated, overcome with gratitude. But he was already moving away, probably uncomfortable at his unusual expression of intimacy.

He had been incredibly kind and given me a new source of courage. But I still felt abandoned by everyone else. I'm not sure what I expected, for there was no question that I had built an invisible curtain around me, but I desperately needed someone to talk to, to lean on, to help me feel better about myself.

As if in answer to my yearnings, Tom was standing outside the hotel when I approached.

"Beth," he called, "I've been waiting for you. I thought for a while you were going to spend the night on the bus."

"Tom," I whispered hoarsely, "I'm so glad you're here."

"Come with me for some coffee. I want to talk to you."

"Oh good, I'm glad somebody wants to."

"I told you there'd be a 'next time' and this is it. You leave in thirty-six hours."

"I know," I sighed, not sure if I was glad or sad after what had happened.

We strolled around the corner and Tom led me to a small cafe that was romantically lit by candles placed in straw-covered Chianti bottles. There were a number of empty tables, and we sat down at one in the corner, ordered two capucinos, and I tried to unwind. At least,

I thought, I have Tom. I was sure he'd say something comforting, but instead he began to tell me about how he was really in hot water with Mr. Saxe.

"He found out about our jaunt to Cambridge, and read me the Riot Act."

"But why did you tell anyone?"

"I just let one person know, for personal reasons."

"For personal reasons?"

"Somebody wanted to know what I was doing on my day off, and I told them."

"Them?"

"I told that person, that's all. Completely innocent slip."

"You had to meet that person later, after you were done with me?"

"Don't be ridiculous, Beth." A flush came over his face, and I knew he was lying, but I didn't want to press him for more information. He was sitting with me now, not Sabrina, and I needed him.

"I'm glad you're here," I said, as though to reassure him and myself that nothing else mattered.

"Me, too, darling. I had to talk to you."

I was sure he was referring to my fiasco, of course he would want to comfort me, and I invited his reassurances.

"Is everyone mad at me?" I asked.

He seemed bewildered by the question, then finally said, "Oh, you mean about tonight."

"Yes, tonight." It was hard for me to believe that anything else could be on his mind.

"No, I don't think they're mad. The Germans have a word for some of the choir's attitude: *Schadenfreude.*"

"What's that mean?" I was in no mood for a language lesson and this did not seem like the appropriate time for Tom to show off his German.

"It means delight in other people's misfortune."

"But that's awful. Why would anyone want to see me fail."

"Well, darling, you do have the best voice, you're obviously Saxe's favorite, and you've got me. You must be perfect."

"That's the last thing I am," I confided miserably. "I feel absolutely awful that I didn't want Greta to sing."

"Let's not talk about it anymore. It's over."

"Not for me, it isn't."

"I refuse to talk about it further. What I want to find out is if I can really visit you in the States next summer."

"I think so," I answered, taken aback by his abrupt shifting of gears and surprised at his insensitivity.

"I'd like to meet your father and perhaps get some advice about my career."

"I'm sure he'd be happy to talk to you, but you have to tell me when."

"Well, the truth is, I thought that between recommendations from my tutors at Cambridge, and knowing you so well, I might be hired by your father's firm for the entire summer."

"You mean you want to visit me so that you'll meet my father, who might give you a job?"

"Something like that. I know if I get the right introductions and get my foot in the door, I'm set."

"And that's why you were so anxious to see me tonight."

"Is there something wrong with that?"

"Tom," I said, my voice quivering, "this has been the worst night of my life. I thought you were waiting for me outside the hotel because you knew how upset I was."

"You're overreacting, Beth. The audience probably

enjoyed the drama—like when the ballerina twists her leg and has to be carried offstage."

"That's not funny."

"It's real, though. And now you've got to go on to other things, just like me. Saxe is so angry with me now—he even blames me for your cold getting worse—that he's writing a letter of complaint to EIE. I couldn't get a job with them again even if I wanted to."

"I think I've heard enough, Tom," I said huskily, shoving away my half-finished cup. I pushed back my chair, and although my head was spinning and my knees liquid, I mustered enough strength to tear out of the restaurant and back to the hotel before Tom could catch up with me.

My room was dark, which meant Daisy was out, but the connecting doors to the bathroom were open, casting an eerie light on the floor. I flopped on the bed, totally forlorn. I had been deceived by Tom and alienated by the chorus, and I had no one to blame but myself.

I became aware of raised voices in the next room—a hot discussion that didn't intrigue me in the least until I heard my name mentioned. Then I almost freaked out. Sabrina, more shrill than usual, was saying, "Beth knew she couldn't sing tonight, but she wouldn't dream of letting anyone else take over."

"Yeah," Helene chimed in, "aren't you mad, Greta?"

"I understand it," Greta said. "Singing means more to Beth than anything."

I wouldn't have blamed Greta for not speaking to me ever again, but here she was defending me. I felt more ashamed and guilty than ever.

"She also thinks she's the queen of all the singers." That was Andy's contribution.

"She didn't realize how bad her throat was, otherwise why would she have taken such a risk?" I recognized Peter's voice, and couldn't believe my ears. He had every right to criticize me, but he was taking my side. He also succeeded in getting them to stop talking about me. Their voices gradually faded and I heard Sabrina say something about not wanting to stay holed up in a room when it was their last chance to see anything of London. Then I heard them leave and close the door.

I went into the bathroom to wash, changed into my nightshirt, and crawled into bed. I wondered if my sore throat had affected my thinking processes because everything was topsy-turvy. Saxe and Greta and Peter, who should have been the most infuriated with me, were the most supportive. Tom, who I had been counting on, couldn't care less. I was overcome with drowsiness, trying to unravel my thoughts.

In the middle of the night, I awoke and felt like I was on fire. For several minutes, I sweated so profusely that I had to get up, rinse off, and change my top. Then I fell back into bed, weak but no longer feverish, and promptly dozed off again.

I didn't wake up until the morning, and I felt remarkably improved. My throat was dry, but no longer painful, and the heaviness in my chest had disappeared. This was the "miracle" cure I had been hoping for—a day late. Even the state of my psyche was better, and I remembered Saxe's words of encouragement, Greta's understanding, and Peter's defense.

Daisy was looking at me as I swung my feet over the side of the bed and I tried to read her expression. She had every right to have an I-told-you-so attitude, to be angry and disappointed, to even stop being my friend.

"You look much better," she observed clinically.

"I am," I said. Then, because I couldn't stand the suspense, I had to know what she thought of me. "Are you still my friend?" I blurted out.

She popped up in bed and looked at me in amazement. "Of course I'm your friend!"

"Even though I didn't listen to you?"

"You made a mistake, Beth, that's all."

"Not just one mistake. I was wrong about Tom, too."

"What do you mean?"

"I flattered myself that he really liked me, taking me to Cambridge and all that. But it turns out he had an ulterior motive. He was using me in order to wangle an invitation to the States, meet my father, and get a job next summer."

"He is handsome and charming, but I never trusted him."

"You're certainly a better judge of character than I am."

"We all make mistakes, Beth."

We smiled comfortably at each other and I knew for sure I'd completely recovered.

12

Patsy, who I expected to make some wisecrack, was amazingly tactful. She charged into our room as we were getting dressed, announced that she and Timmy were giving each other the morning off, and casually asked me how I felt.

"She's fine," Daisy answered for me.

"But she can't talk, and that's why you're answering for her," Patsy chided Daisy.

"I really am fine," I said. "It burned itself out last night."

"Actually, you do sound perfect," Patsy observed. "You'll be able to sing tonight." She sounded delighted.

"But I'm not going to."

"Why not?" Daisy asked. "You've wanted to sing tonight more than anything."

"Not anymore. More than anything, I want Greta to take my place."

"Beth, you look normal, you sound normal, but I think the mind's gone," Patsy commented.

"Please," I pleaded, "it may sound crazy, but I don't want Mr. Saxe to know I got my voice back. If he finds out, he'll want me to sing, and I really don't want to. I owe something to Greta, and you've got to help me."

Patsy and Daisy raised their eyebrows at each other, then looked at me and shook their heads.

"Please," I urged, "do this for me."

Daisy sighed, "She's serious, Patsy, she really doesn't want to sing tonight."

"Then we won't let her," Patsy stated in her most positive manner.

"But you better fake that husky voice," Daisy advised. "It sounds clear as a bell."

"Don't worry. I'm going to tell Mr. Saxe first thing this morning in my most gravelly tones." I pitched my voice down to my shoes and croaked, "I can't sing."

"Don't overdo it," Patsy laughed, "or he might send you to the hospital."

The rest of the morning Daisy and Patsy hung out with me like bodyguards. Whenever anyone came over to talk to me—I was amazed at how many kids were genuinely interested in how I was feeling—they answered for me. I had no trouble convincing Mr. Saxe that I'd have to be a listener for the final concert. He even suggested that I rest all day so that I'd be able to be part of the audience at night.

During the rehearsal that afternoon, I messed around in my room, repacking, reading one of the three paperbacks that I hadn't cracked since the trip began, and taking advantage of the empty bathroom to shower and shampoo. The enforced rest made me feel better than ever, and I had to really put on a "sick" act during dinner. It was difficult, because everyone was enormously high, anticipating the evening concert at the Rivers Parish Church where all the ancestors of the Eleventh Earl of Rivers are buried.

The atmosphere during the bus ride to the church was charged with nervous anticipation. Our final and most important concert, combined with the knowledge that this was the end of the tour, made everyone slightly unhinged. It wasn't easy not to participate in the banter, but I forced myself to remain silent, and when we arrived at the church, I made a special point of sitting far back by myself. I didn't want to be next to Julie and Clyde, much as I liked them, for fear I couldn't keep up my sick front.

I watched the people file into the church and tried not to feel so disembodied. I know this sounds spacey, but my body was in the audience and my heart and soul was with the choir. I had never heard them from the vantage point of the audience, and when the concert began, I was overwhelmed with the quality of the singing. Greta's solo was superb, and elicited a clamorous response from the audience. It was her moment, well-deserved, and I felt strangely responsible.

When the concert was over, I wandered outside, waiting for the others. Greta was one of the first to appear, and must have been looking for me. She dashed over to where I was standing, threw her arms around me, and said, "Was I okay?"

"You were fantastic," I told her, totally forgetting my sore throat act. "I can't believe how musical you are."

"Thank goodness," she cried. "I knew you'd tell me the truth."

"I couldn't have done it any better."

Greta looked at me, stunned, and then said, "Yes,

you could have. Your voice has come back. Why didn't you tell Mr. Saxe?"

"There was no guarantee."

"But you sound perfectly normal."

The rest of the choir had come out of the church and were crowding around Greta, congratulating her and themselves, and herding her onto the bus. She continued to look at me in astonishment, and I couldn't help chuckling to myself at her total bewilderment. I was sure she would not reveal my secret, but I still had to get through the reception at Rivers Manor, the residence of Lady Rivers, who was a distant cousin of Jeremy's.

It was a short distance from the church to Lady Rivers's enormous, opulent Tudor home. Lady Rivers, a gray-haired eminence, wearing a flamboyant black-beaded gown, greeted us effusively and led us into the dining hall where a large banquet table was filled with fruits, cheeses, tea sandwiches, and as a concession to our American tastes, pizza and soft drinks.

"Before you partake of these refreshments," Tom told us, "Dr. Jeremy Rivers would like to say a few words."

"I'll be brief," Dr. Rivers promised, "but I want you to know that tonight's concert was a culmination of a lifelong dream. I want to thank Mr. Saxe and the Bryant High School choir for making it happen."

We cheered and hollered for such a long time that Dr. Rivers finally raised his hands to quiet us down. "Please," he begged, "you'll disappoint my cousin, Lady Rivers, and you'll not live up to your reputation, if you don't immediately plunge into the refreshments."

That was all we needed to plow into the food, and

after some serious eating, Mr. Saxe rapped on the table for our attention.

"Lady Rivers, who is a patron of the arts and a fine pianist, would like to accompany our soloist in an aria from *Madame Butterfly*, 'Un Bel Di.'"

"I would be so thrilled," Lady Rivers enthused. "If you'll just follow me into the music room. I think there are enough seats to accommodate all of us."

We seated ourselves on red velvet-covered chairs, while Greta took her place at the piano. The bronze statuary standing in the corners, and the paintings of the present Rivers forebears that graced the walls, provided the room with an old-world elegance. I was absorbed in looking at a painting of a distinguished-looking frock-coated Rivers ancestor when I heard Greta say, "I don't know this aria, but Beth does, and I'm sure she wouldn't want to disappoint Lady Rivers."

There were gasps and whispers and mumblings, and I was in a state of shock. Then I felt a distinct push from Daisy and Patsy, who were seated on either side of me.

"Go ahead," Daisy urged in a low voice.

"You've got to," Patsy insisted.

I moved toward the piano, almost in a daze, nodded to Lady Rivers, and then turning toward the group, proceeded to sing literally from the heart. When the aria was finished, there was silence, and I was terrified that I had deceived myself about my performance. But then I heard deafening applause and Lady Rivers was actually kissing me on the cheek and murmuring, "Exquisite, my dear."

The next thing I knew, Tom was beside me. He hadn't paid any attention to me all day, so I was surprised when he asked me if I'd like to see the balcony of the Rivers Manor.

"What do you want," I asked as sweetly as possible.

"I want to explain to you about last night. I was wrong. . . ."

"I was wrong, Tom," I interrupted.

"You were?" He looked at me eagerly, probably expecting me to apologize for my childish behavior, running away without an explanation.

"Yes, very wrong."

"About what, darling? Tell me." He was all smiles.

"I thought you were, as the British say, the bee's knees."

"And now?" He looked at me expectantly.

"And now, as the Americans say, I think you're the pits!"

If I had struck him physically, he could not have looked more astounded. The color drained from his face and his mouth opened and closed, but no sounds emerged. I walked off triumphantly, convinced that this was the first time Tom was ever speechless.

I wasn't sure where I was going, but Evan blocked my way. After praising my performance, he began to explain the geneology of the Rivers family as represented by the family portraits. As he droned on, I looked around the room, trying to find the one person I *had* to talk to—Peter. I finally noticed he was in a huddle in the corner with Patsy and Daisy. Even if I could have edged my way away from Evan, it would have been rude for me to barge in on their conversation. I'd just have to wait.

I tried to tune in on what Evan was saying, but just as I was about to find an excuse to leave, Clyde and Julie went into their party-is-over routine. I bid goodbye to Lady Rivers and Dr. Jeremy, and with their compliments buzzing in my head, I drifted toward the bus. I was so deep in thought, thinking that this was our last concert, our last bus ride—except for the one to the airport—and our last night of being together in London, that I wasn't aware of anyone trying to catch up with me until I felt a tap on my shoulder.

"Beth, I've got to talk to you." It was Peter, and my heart unexpectedly was racing.

"I know," I said, "I mean I've got to talk to *you*."

"I can't sit with you on the bus because Kiki's been bugging me to give her advice about being a music major. I promised I'd tell her everything I knew before we fly back home, and this is my last chance. I'll leave my music in my room and meet you in the lobby."

"Terrific," I said smiling, secretly relieved that it wasn't Pris he had to advise.

Peter dumped his music in his room and I changed into my pink sweater and skirt. I always thought Peter was shy around girls, but as we left the hotel he took my hand so naturally I thought I must have misjudged him. He said, "Let's walk down the next street. There's a bench that's right in front of a church there, and we can sit down."

"Sounds good," I agreed. "I've been trying to talk to you alone ever since last night."

"What have I done?" he asked.

"I wanted to thank you for taking my side last night."

"How did you know I took your side?"

"I was in my room, but nobody knew it, and I heard the whole conversation. That was really terrific of you, especially after you'd tried to talk me out of singing."

"I was only telling them the truth."

"Also, you were right about that phony English charm. I found out the hard way, but now I'm completely turned off."

"Maybe I should be a psychologist instead of a

musician," he laughed. "I seem to be shelling out a lot of advice lately, not that anyone ever listens."

"I'm going to listen from here on in," I promised, "if it's not too late."

"Why should it be?" We had arrived at the bench in front of the church and sat down.

"Well," I said quickly, before I lost my nerve, "what about Pris?"

"Pris? Pris?" he repeated.

"Everytime I looked at you, you were with her." I tried to keep the edge out of my voice.

"I happen to think Pris is great, but I don't love *her*."

"Are you trying to tell me something, Peter?" My stomach seemed to suddenly flip-flop.

He smiled at me and said, "For a girl who doesn't know when she shouldn't sing, and doesn't know when she's being taken advantage of by an ambitious Cambridge law student, you're remarkably perceptive about me."

Then he folded both arms around me, and kissed me, tenderly at first, and then with more and more urgency. We clutched each other for minutes, and I never felt more secure, protected, and attuned to anyone in my life. Finally he pulled away and traced my face gently with his fingertips.

"I'll never forget this moment," he said, "but we must leave."

"'Fraid so," I muttered. "We can't spend the night on this bench."

"There are some kids I promised I'd meet in the party room, you know the one, just off the dining room. We thought we'd have one final blast. You'll come with me, of course."

"Of course," I said, as we both stood up.

We ambled back to the hotel, his arm around me,

thinking our own thoughts. I couldn't believe how much had happened to me in these three weeks. I'd experienced so many things and so many emotions, more intensely than I ever expected I would again. Love, hate, jealousy, friendship, loyalty, art, dedication, foolishness. I knew, also, that I had invited a lot of intense feelings, not always friendly. I couldn't blame a lot of people for being hostile. As Tom had said, "You have the best voice, your Saxe's pet, and you have me." That was some people's perception, even if it wasn't true.

"Hey, we're here, Beth," Peter said, as I started to walk past our hotel. "You were really far away."

"You've rescued me once again," I told him, as I stopped short and turned into the lobby.

There was a lot of noise in the party room, but it abated dramatically as I stepped across the threshold. It seemed the entire choir was seated at a long banquet table, drinking colas. I felt really weird, as though I'd intruded on some secret society, and instinctively backed away. But Peter was behind me, blocking my exit.

Then Mr. Saxe stood up, and said, "This tour has meant something different to each one of us. It's been an unique experience, and I don't think any of us knows the impact it will have on our lives. I'm not one to make speeches, but tonight I feel impelled to tell you what a great choir you are, what remarkable singers, but more than that, what fine human beings. No one symbolizes what I'm trying to say better than Beth. We've always known how much music there is in her, but now we know it is equaled by her humanity."

I was frozen, unable to move, while the room vibrated with everyone giving me a standing ovation. Then the tears that I thought were permanently buried, welled up and poured down my face. Images of all we'd experienced, from that first night on the Thames to the final reception at Lady Rivers's, flashed through my mind. It was almost too much to grasp, but more than anything I knew this had been not just a tour of England, but a tour of discovery.

Three exciting First Love from Silhouette romances yours for 15 days—_free!_

If you enjoyed this First Love from Silhouette® you'll want to read more! These are true-to-life romances about the things that matter most to you now—your friendships, dating, getting along in school, and learning about yourself. The stories could really happen, and the characters are so real they'll seem like friends.

Now you can get 3 First Love from Silhouette romances to look over for 15 days—absolutely free! If you decide not to keep them, simply return them and pay nothing. But if you enjoy them as much as we believe you will, keep them and pay the invoice enclosed with your trial shipment. You'll then become a member of the First Love from Silhouette℠ Book Club and will receive 3 more new First Love from Silhouette romances every month. You'll always be among the first to get them, and you'll never miss a new title. There is no minimum number of books to buy and you can cancel at any time. To receive your 3 books, mail the coupon below today.

First Love from Silhouette® is a service mark and a registered trademark of Simon & Schuster.

First Love from Silhouette

THERE'S NOTHING QUITE AS SPECIAL AS A FIRST LOVE.

$1.75 each

2 ☐ GIRL IN THE ROUGH
Wunsch

3 ☐ PLEASE LET ME IN
Beckman

4 ☐ SERENADE
Marceau

6 ☐ KATE HERSELF
Erskine

7 ☐ SONGBIRD
Enfield

14 ☐ PROMISED KISS
Ladd

15 ☐ SUMMER ROMANCE
Diamond

16 ☐ SOMEONE TO LOVE
Bryan

17 ☐ GOLDEN GIRL
Erskine

18 ☐ WE BELONG TOGETHER
Harper

19 ☐ TOMORROW'S WISH
Ryan

20 ☐ SAY PLEASE!
Francis

$1.95 each

24 ☐ DREAM LOVER
Treadwell

26 ☐ A TIME FOR US
Ryan

27 ☐ A SECRET PLACE
Francis

29 ☐ FOR THE LOVE OF LORI
Ladd

30 ☐ A BOY TO DREAM ABOUT
Quinn

31 ☐ THE FIRST ACT
London

32 ☐ DARE TO LOVE
Bush

33 ☐ YOU AND ME
Johnson

34 ☐ THE PERFECT FIGURE
March

35 ☐ PEOPLE LIKE US
Haynes

36 ☐ ONE ON ONE
Ketter

37 ☐ LOVE NOTE
Howell

First Love from Silhouette

38 ☐ ALL-AMERICAN GIRL
   Payton

39 ☐ BE MY VALENTINE
   Harper

40 ☐ MY LUCKY STAR
   Cassiday

41 ☐ JUST FRIENDS
   Francis

42 ☐ PROMISES TO COME
   Dellin

43 ☐ A KNIGHT TO REMEMBER
   Martin

44 ☐ SOMEONE LIKE
   JEREMY VAUGHN
   Alexander

45 ☐ A TOUCH OF LOVE
   Madison

46 ☐ SEALED WITH A KISS
   Davis

47 ☐ THREE WEEKS OF LOVE
   Aks

48 ☐ SUMMER ILLUSION
   Manning

49 ☐ ONE OF A KIND
   Brett

SPRING INTO ROMANCE THIS JUNE WITH FRAN FISHER'S
STAY, SWEET LOVE

FIRST LOVE, Department FL/4
1230 Avenue of the Americas
New York, NY 10020

Please send me the books I have checked above. I am enclosing $_____ (please add 50¢ to cover postage and handling. NYS and NYC residents please add appropriate sales tax). Send check or money order—no cash or C.O.D.'s please. Allow six weeks for delivery.

NAME _____

ADDRESS _____

CITY_____ STATE/ZIP_____

First Love from Silhouette

Coming Next Month

Stay, Sweet Love

Fran Fisher

Island girls usually never again heard from their summer sweethearts after the ferries had carried them to the mainland. Only Ellen knew that Rob, her first sweet love, would return to her as surely as the tides washed in and the moon rose.

Prairie Girl

Barbara Coy

Stephanie hated moving to her grandmother's isolated farm in Oklahoma. That was before she fell under the spell of rolling mountains and windswept prairies, before she met a tall, dark-haired boy as rugged and exciting as the vast country she grew to love.

A Summer To Remember

Carol Robertson

Fun filled weeks at Fire Island . . . the best looking guy in the summer crowd as a tennis partner . . . would it be a love match or just a passing game?

Silhouette **Romance**

15-Day Free Trial Offer
6 Silhouette Romances

6 Silhouette Romances, free for 15 days! We'll send you 6 new Silhouette Romances to keep for 15 days, absolutely free! If you decide not to keep them, send them back to us. You pay nothing.

Free Home Delivery. But if you enjoy them as much as we think you will, keep them by paying the invoice enclosed with your free trial shipment. We'll pay all shipping and handling charges. You get the convenience of Home Delivery and we pay the postage and handling charge each month.

Don't miss a copy. The Silhouette Book Club is the way to make sure you'll be able to receive every new romance we publish before they're sold out. There is no minimum number of books to buy and you can cancel at any time.